Praise for worl

from new readers of all

Breaking The Rules

Love, love, love your new book! You retained your ability to paint wonderful pictures with words and gave remarkable descriptions while doing it more succinctly. I was mesmerized for hours! This is the type of adventure teens long for!

Carola Smail
Speech Language Pathologist in Federal Way
Public Schools, WA
Auburn, WA

I read software, business and technical subject matters but do not make a practice of reading fiction. I, however, look forward to reading virdean's books

Steve Kenzell
Software Engineer
Seattle, WA

Action, mystery and humor are packed into this colorful unraveled survival story. "Breaking The Rules" vividly pulls the reader back into the mysterious adventures of Sebastian Boyle. Eager for more!

Jennifer Hall
Digital Media Manager at Realty Marketing/Northwest
Portland, OR

I always enjoy a mystery, especially with all the intrigue as this writer has put forth.

Ron Eastley
Senior Citizen
Puyallup, WA

Breaking
The
Rules

*A High School
Mystery*

Works by virdean:

Changing The Rules (A Sebastian thriller)

A Bad Day

A Wilderness Night Scare

A Politically Correct 4th Grader

Caught

People Can Be Mean

The Runaway Torpedo

Unlucky

These items may be purchased at www.virdean.com or direct from the author at the address noted on page 241

BREAKING

THE

RULES

A Senior High School

Mystery

by

virdean

Puyallup, WA

Photo Credits: Carola Smail, thesimpleartist.com (front cover), virdean (back cover)

Front and back cover by virdean

Artwork by virdean

Editors: Virginia Hartzell, Carola Smail

To the Emerald Ridge High School Staff who each year are rewarded when they see the results of their dedication to developing strong intelligent citizens. The purpose of this writing is to show first hand the challenges of their endeavor.

Also, this work is for the United States servicemen who are dedicating their lives to provide protection for us.

<u>Be careful, The truth is not always told.</u>

"I have a grander standard of principle than George Washington. He could not lie, but I won't." Samuel Clemens

You don't know about me unless you have read a book by the name of *Changing The Rules;* but that is okay. That book was made by the same author, *virdean*, and he told the truth for the most part. There were things that were stretched, but mainly you could count on what he said. This adds to that story but is self-contained--that is, you will be up to speed as you read this story. The difference is, I am older now and the affairs that come my way protract me beyond my abilities. I must break the rules.

This story is written in the setting of a local Puyallup, Washington community. Several places, Emerald Ridge High School, streets, Fred Meyer, and the Chevron station exist and can be seen by visiting South Hill. However, this is a work of fiction for reading pleasure. Names and references are invented and used purely for entertainment without intent to create ridicule, offense or malice.

"The Old believe everything;

the Middle-aged suspect everything;

and the Young know everything."

Oscar Wilde

Although this is fiction, it may be

that you are old enough to believe

everything, or maybe you are at the

age where not one crumb is true.

Table of Contents

List of Characters

Aflakian, Amin	Iranian student
Boyle, Sebastian	Emerald Ridge HS sophomore
Burbank, Mr.	Emerald Ridge HS Math teacher
Campbell, Hugh	Stahl JHS Principal
Comfort, Sheila	girl friend
Diangello, Angeline	purse owner
Diangello, Ron (Hangman)	from Devoreaux
Diangello, Wilbur (Caterpillar Eyes)	from Devoreaux
Espinoza, Jel	Emerald Ridge HS Senior
Espinoza, Juan	Emerald Ridge HS Sophomore
Finn James,	Emerald Ridge HS principal
Graves, Mr.	Emerald Ridge HS Civics' teacher
Newton, John	U.S. Army Staff Sergeant
Whitney, Lynn	girl with spotted skirt
Trimbell, Mrs.	Emerald Ridge HS English teacher
Vera, Agent Abernathy	Seattle Homeland Security agent
Ward, John	John Newton's friend
Webster, Ms. Hazel	Emerald Ridge HS assistant principal
Weeback, Mrs.	Devoreaux lady
Whitney, Lynn	missing girl with spotted skirt

Prologue

Mid-fall 2010

"Principal Finn. Can I squeeze in for a minute?" inquired Ms. Webster, one of three assistant principals at Emerald Ridge High School in Puyallup.

Needing time to report the recent cherry bomb incident to the school board, Principal James Finn was in his office by 5 A.M. Ms. Webster's disturbing interruption stalled him before he could start.

"What's she doing here at this ungodly hour?" he wondered but feared the answer, if he asked.

"After yesterday's fiasco, I came in at 3 A.M. to act as a watchman in case someone came back. I used the time to review yesterday's reports. Something was overlooked. A custodian reported a missing five gallon can of white paint which was found outside the office door. I thought that you might want to include it in the report you submit to the police and school board.

"By the way, not a soul has been around until you came in. Sorry for the interruption."

"Thank you for your diligence and concern for the report, Ms. Webster. Yes, I will include the relocated paint. I'm curious, why the paint?"

"On NCIS last week, an intruder covered his tracks by pouring paint behind him as he left."

"Maybe so. That must mean our thief may have walked across the sandy football field to get in.

"Would you put the 'Do Not Disturb' sign on the door as you leave? Thank you."

Part I

Fall

Each of us selects his own path.

When nothing seems to work, bending the rules may help. If that fails, look to changing the rules. Even if tempted, avoid breaking the rules.

1 | *Visitors*

I immediately dropped to the floor and crawled behind the couch out of sight. Homeland Security Agent Abernathy Vera's warning "you should avoid tangling with them for your own and your family's safety" tumbled through my mind like a warning bell clanging at a railroad crossing. Those two Hyundai guys at the door, the Diangello brothers, would resort to anything and I knew revenge was their sweetest, favorite dessert. I was sure that they were now aware that the money was gone, known to be over $3,000,000. They were here for clues on how to get it back

Kneeling behind the couch, I was hardly able to catch my breath as I heard a deep growl from the door invade the living room. My mind dwelt on how to protect my clueless family and prevent my own exposure to them. Memories of the last nine months clouded my thinking.

It started in January when I caught sight of an accelerating Hyundai racing my way. I, Sebastian Boyle, a 9th grade student, had to leap from the street and sidewalk in fear for my life when the vehicle plunged towards me. As the car squeezed by, a woman's brown, almost black, purse was thrown out and clipped my hood. The shotgun passenger must have seen it smack me and watched where the purse had landed.

Now, unexpectedly and uninvited, these two were at my door, wanting to question me, the "struck" bystander. After that January event, they had repeatedly stalked me. The two had frightened a volunteer office clerk so badly that she feared for her life when they invaded the school office looking for me. They had terrified my mother with a surprise "drop-in" while she was alone during the day. Still without answers, here they were at my home on this "late-after-hours" visit. Their intent could not be good.

Features of each were enough to make my dad take two steps back. But Dad's feet stayed anchored. He bent his knees slightly and bowed his body forward as a football lineman preparing for the center to hike the ball. After working as a boy with 2000 pound Texas long-horns, my dad was no slouch at six foot two and wasn't intimidated easily. He refused to back away from those greater than he, be it a steer or a man. But the shocking double-intimidation facing him must have taken his breath away.

The tall one, closer to seven than six feet, had opened his lantern jaw like a barracuda shark as he growled. He raised his caterpillar eyebrows to clear his vision, and pierced his blue Siberian Husky eyes over my dad's shoulder, scanning the room.

The short one was letting the big guy lead the charge. His hangman's face, squinty eyes, long curled down mustache and goatee beard portrayed a scowl that told it all, a face that had more lines than a road map. He scared me the most. As a class assignment, I had recently read *The Pride and the Sorrow,* a story of mayhem about a hangman in English history, and this guy was a twin of what I had imagined.

Seeing these two so close for the first time fried my thoughts and they stuck together in my head like socks clinging together without Cling Free. Doing my best, I tried to sort out what I should do, perhaps a miracle. All I could focus on was my nick-naming game--"Caterpillar Eyebrows" and "Hangman".

Recall of their stalking presence for so long was fresher than the Mariner baseball game that I'd just been watching on TV. Each of those past glimpses of them swirled through my mind. Remembering their pursuit during all that time, I was convinced that these guys were certain that I had picked up the purse.

Yes, after a search in the cold rain, I found the purse, a purse which contained access information to a $3,000,000 account in a Cayman Island bank. Following discovery of its contents, I concealed the purse while I sought to return it to its rightful owner. The purse belonged to their sister-in-law, Angeline Diangello, who was held under house arrest for seven months by this horrible pair.

Although the two Hyundai men, Hyundai because their car

seemed to be a part of their attire, probably weren't positive that I had the purse, I was their only link and they had relentlessly haunted me. Here they were, brassily affronting my family. With the details I knew of their history, I expected them to go to any extreme, maybe even resort to torture or a kidnapping.

Brushing my five inch locks behind my ears, I poked my head around the corner of the couch, my chin brushing the floor. The two were standing outside on the porch landing. Dad was obstructing their view. I could crawl on hands and knees, out of sight, through the hall to my room and exit through my bedroom window. Mom, rising from her rocker, approached the front door to join Dad. With both Mom and Dad hampering their view, I wormed unseen from the couch into the hall.

"They're Pierce County Sheriff Detectives. They were here before wanting to talk to Sebastian. Have them come in. I'll go get Sebastian," I heard Mom say as I scooted down the hall.

My plan to use my bedroom window flew away like a July 4th rocket. Without waiting, after hearing my mother, they immediately powered their way past Dad. My mother had sauntered to the hall to find me. With her coming, there wasn't enough time for my bedroom window escape. I instead entered Mom and Dad's bedroom and gently closed the door. Mom would spend a few seconds searching my room and then the bathroom. I had time for a call. As a trainee on a Homeland Security task force, I had access to a fast response team.

Dialing a friend, Homeland Security Agent Vera, I

scrunched to the floor behind the bed hoping to avoid being heard.

"Homeland Security, Agent Vera."

"Sebastian here. The Diangello clowns are here in my house. What do I do?"

"Stall them. I'll have a Pierce County deputy there in five minutes. I'm close by, in Edgewood, and I'll be there in 15," and the connection broke.

Regaining my confidence, I replaced the phone and started for the bedroom door. Bad timing. The bedroom door whacked open against the wall, breaking the doorstop. Another step and I would have been on the floor with a bloody nose and black eye.

"I thought I heard your voice in here. I've been looking all over for you. What in the world are you doing in here?" demanded Mom as she whipped her vision through the room to see what I had been into. Satisfied, she whirled to confront me, her hair falling into her eyes as she swung her head.

"I had to use the phone. There was no privacy out there so I used this one."

"Come on. Two policemen are here to see you. Wait... no...you go on, give me a couple of minutes." Then she stopped to fix her hair and pretty her face for the company. It was my bet that she'd exchange jeans for a dress. If she only knew.

I sauntered into the hallway. Using an age old trick to tally time, I counted seconds 1001, 1002, 1003...hoping that I could hold out to 1300, a five minute 60 second count, when help would arrive. Passing the bathroom, I knew another minute could be consumed in there so I went in.

With the count at 1120, down to three remaining minutes, I meandered down the hall to the living room. Dad stood at the end of the hall facing the living room, deliberately blocking access beyond the hall. Something had raised a red flag and I saw what it was. Beyond Dad, the two men were also standing; both dressed in black suits, white shirts, black ties, and black shoes. Caterpillar Eyebrows was at the front door and Hangman was at the kitchen door. Bad sign! They were plugging the exits!

"These guys want to take you to the 'station' and I said, 'no way.' Then the short one pulled a pistol," was my father's suppressed murmur to me as I touched his back.

My scalp tingled when I looked at the Hangman's face. His curled down mustache was bobbing about his goatee as he worked his tongue across his lips. He had a hungry look like you get from not eating for a while. And I would be the salad, the first course.

I actually felt the hair on the back of head rise. The tension was electric. My little sister Sarah, asleep in her room, was probably safe. My Mom was still gone, so it was just Dad and I.

"Dad, let me talk to these guys and find what they want. Okay?"

Hearing my voice, the Hangman, at the kitchen door, lifted his pistol and waved it to and fro. He was like a four year old who had found his father's gun too heavy to hold erect and aim.

"You're Shebashtian? Nobody movesh a mushcle until we get shome anshwersh," he blurted with a lisp.

My dad had his own rules. "Sebastian, you can talk but stay behind me," he ordered. He had the telephone book in his right hand, held as a cleaver, and a long vase in his left, clutched like an ax when chopping wood. The carpet was covered with puddles and flowers.

"Who are you?" I bravely queried.

"I'm Piershe County Sheriff Detective Diangello and so ish he; he'sh my brother," spoke Hangman, confusing me with his *c* and *s's*. I knew better as I remembered their claim to be university representatives during a Stahl Junior High school office visit in the spring.

Stalling for time, I asked, "I've seen you traipsing around for nine months. Can I see some ID, please?"

How much longer? I had failed to keep count but five minutes must be long gone.

"We're off duty and we're on our way home. We left our credentials at the station," replied Caterpillar Eyebrows.

Stall. Stall. Stall. Help is on the way.

My fear was to the point that my voice shook as I asked questions. Hearing the quaver in my speech, Dad mumbled, "It's okay, two of them, two of us. If they make a move, we'll start things. As big as you are, you can handle the short one with the pistol at the kitchen door. Grab the floor lamp, use it as a spear-- I'll be after the tall one. Don't let the pistol fool you. See how he waves it? He doesn't know how to use it, let alone aim it. The safety is still on."

With the encouragement of Dad's words, I blurted, "Do you have anything to show who you are? A driver's license or a visa credit card with a photo would do."

Both reached for their wallets, one to a breast pocket like a kangaroo. The other put his hand to the right rear but snagged it on the holster's bulge there. Neither was having success and both Dad and I could see that they were dilly-dallying.

I heard a car stop quietly two doors down and hoped that the authorities had come. Moments were all that were left. The car had approached in a silent, lights-off mode--the crack in the window drapes had remained dark--so I still wished that I was right and they were finally here.

"Dad, let's forget the ID. Let me find out what these guys want."

I stuck my head out a little farther. "What do you want?"

"I'll ask it again. Are you Sebastian?" Caterpillar Eyebrows growled, his growl deeper than that of the Doberman next door.

"You know my name? Yes, I'm Sebastian."

"Were you at the school bus stop next door, the first day of school in 2009?"

"Yes."

"Did you see a woman's purse while you were there?"

From events that occurred during my last year at Stahl Junior High, I was professionally trained to use a bit of truth to mislead. I thought that one more stall would be enough while I waited for the doorbell.

"Yeah, maybe."

Their eyes flashed like a mountain lion's in the night just beyond the periphery of a campfire. Hangman pointed his wavering pistol at me and the ugly one grasped and raised his pistol from the holster.

A melody of the Star Spangled Banner chimed, the doorbell's call for attention. It was as if a flash freeze had blown in; frozen silence engulfed us.

"Nobody move. Wait for them to go away," the ugly guy, Caterpillar Eyebrows, ordered. Who put him in charge? My thoughts tumbled in my head, banging around like my shoes when I throw them in the washer. A knock, ker-wump, ker-wump, walloping on the door broke the spell.

"Police! Open up!"

Holding my breath and betting that the pair would not shoot their only link to the purse, I broke the tall ugly guy's rules. I ducked under my Dad's protective arm, walked directly toward Caterpillar Eyebrows daring him to shoot and then past him to open the door. Before me were two Pierce County Sheriff deputies, name tags clearly showing and officially identifying them. I waved them in.

Clunk! Hangman had dropped his pistol to conceal it under his foot. Caterpillar Eyebrows jerked his pistol to hide it behind his back.

"Please come in, Officers. You're welcome here any time,"

I invited. "But before I get to the purpose of your call, I want to deal with these two; they were first."

Spinning to look at the Diangellos, I said, "You identified yourselves as Pierce County Sheriff detectives. Then you asked if I saw a woman's purse while I was at the bus stop the first school day in January. Yes, I did. Fact is, it hit me." Those few words should bring the newly arrived deputies up to speed. The uniformed deputies, clearing the front door, sized up the Diangellos.

"Can we see your ID, please?" the younger said as he scrutinized Caterpillar Eyebrows and then Hangman.

An un-earthy breath emerged from the Diangellos. The situation had become eerie the moment that the door opened. Their names and addresses would become public domain as soon as they handed over the wallets. Again the dilly-dallying show started. This time though, wallets came out and were handed to the deputies.

"Ron and Wilbur Diangello from over here in Devoreaux? We had a noise complaint last spring about you. Now you are impersonating an officer?" Detecting the holster bulges, the younger officer went on.

"Do you have a license to carry concealed weapons?" John Dupree, per his nametag, demanded. Young to be a policeman, he was all business, probably a recent academy graduate. He had spread his feet, bent his knees, stooped to a standard police attack stance and placed his hand on his weapon. I could see that he was on edge. He flicked his badge to be sure that it was visible.

```
┌─────────────────────────────────────┐
│                                      │
│        Pierce County Sheriff         │
│        Deputy John Dupree            │
│                 123                  │
│                                      │
└─────────────────────────────────────┘
```

The gray-haired deputy, clean cut except for muddy shoes, lifted his weapon and spoke to his partner, "Pick up their weapons. We'll have to take them in and book them."

Muddy shoes? He must have tramped in Mom's fresh front flower patch trying to see through the window. He was in trouble on two scores, wrecked flowers and mud tracks on the carpet.

Things were moving too fast. I wanted Wonder Woman, Agent Vera, to be in on this.

"Hey, I don't want these guys coming back," I said with the intent to prevent their immediate departure. "Let me answer their questions before they have to go." That was a joke: They'd never stop coming back.

"We'd all like to hear the answers. Go ahead," agreed Dad.

"You saw a woman's purse?" Caterpillar Eyebrows queried.

"Well, I'm not sure. It might have been a glove or something else. It was black or brown and was kind of hard to see, lying over behind the bushes. I had missed my bus and I didn't want to take the time in the storm to look, so I left it where it was. When I came home, it was gone. I assumed that it was picked up by the neighbors."

How is that for a tale? This was getting to be fun. Would I ever return to being a naïve, innocent, honest, honorable young man? Here I was, bold-faced lying in front of police, Diangellos, and Dad. Sensing a hand on my back, I crooked my head and there stood Mom in a dress.

A little knowledge is not a good thing. It can do a lot of damage. Mom, with the little she knew, would not be left out.

"But you did say you found a purse and returned it when that lady called to say thank you," injected my Mom.

Ouch. Caught flat-footed with my bold-face lies, I went over and sat on the couch, pretending deep thought to recall. "You mean when that lady called on that Saturday afternoon when I had been helping down at the school?"

"Yes, that's the time," and Mom nodded.

One lie begets another. I swallowed once and then again. I couldn't clear the dryness. I coughed but that didn't help. I hacked and that made it worse. The swells of saliva had dried in my mouth and I wondered if I would have to excuse myself. The delay allowed me to draw a response. I found my voice.

"That was from last summer. Actually, she was an old lady and she didn't lose her purse. It just fell off the back of a bench. I spotted it there under the bush when I went by and handed it to her. She was looking for it while sitting on the bench and was too stiff to put her head down and see it." Would I ever quit? But what else could I do? Telling the truth was not the way out.

Back to the Diangellos, I continued with falsehoods.

"Sorry but I can't give you any more information. I thought I saw it in the morning rain, but it wasn't there at night, so I may have imagined it. That's all I know."

The truth was, as I stated earlier, I had been hit by the purse, found it, willfully kept it from the Diangello brothers and routed it to the rightful owner through Homeland Security Agent Vera. And the rightful owner, the Diangellos' sister (now released from house arrest), was the caller who Mom had referred to.

Another cycle of the Star Spangled Banner chimed.

That had to be Agent Vera. I raced to the door and let her in. She could see my relief to see her and gave me a one-toothed smile. She hadn't changed. Her face was soft pink without weather exposure and her hair was gray streaked and glazed like a Krispy-Kreme with wild tufts over each ear. She was beautiful compared to Hangman and Caterpillar Eyebrows.

"Let the party begin. I'm here," she whispered to me. Showing her badge, she alerted the deputies that she would take it from here.

Muddy Shoes objected saying, "But carrying concealed weapons without a license and impersonating an officer..."

Agent Vera cut him off. "We have bigger fish to fry. It would be a waste our time and money to book these guys on something that would end with putting the county under a load of legal action. They have powerful friends and would be out before papers could be filed. Let me handle it. Thank you for your help."

The deputies left grumbling. I pulled the drapes and

watched them jaw all the way to their car. Disputing their freeze-out of what appeared to be a high-credit arrest, the deputies were angry and didn't want to leave. This was their jurisdiction and they perceived that there may be a chance that they could override the Homeland Security take-over. They continued bickering in their idling car, trying to work it out.

Agent Vera took the Diangellos to their car and after a few words, the brothers roared off. In a day or two, they would realize that I had called authorities and had fibbed. They would be back like E. coli bacteria searching for a warm side of beef. Yes, they would be back and my dwelling hibernating paranoia could imagine them kidnapping me or someone in my family.

The deputies, seeing the Diangellos' hasty departure, followed, hoping to nail them with a traffic violation.

Relieved to see the party over, I watched each group leave. Slowly ambling toward her car and stopping at the bumper, Agent Vera hesitated as if she was trying to recall what she might have forgotten. She then whirled and purposely marched, arms swinging, for the front door.

2 | *A Cherry Bomb*

The consternation in Agent Vera's face as she neared the house alerted me that my night wasn't over. I opened the door for her and she asked Mom and Dad to find a way to be comfortable. She addressed me with, "Sebastian you had better stay."

She pulled a stool from the kitchen so she could look down on us and began.

"Apparently the Diangello situation is not going away. You are all potential victims of their misdeeds. I don't have the authority to reveal the Diangellos' case histories. However, I can tell you that it would be a violation of National Security if I did."

National Security? That seized Mom and Dad's attention. Both pairs of eyes glued to me. Without speaking, they were asking, "What have you gotten us into?"

"Sebastian, I think that it is time I lifted the clamp from your lips and filled in your parents on what you have been through. Having them know is for their safety." And she told the Diangellos' story.

As her words came out, heaviness in the atmosphere began to build like a low-level nagging headache. The lies about the old woman on the bench and the purse kept popping up like maggots fried in hot grease. My character was torn to shreds with each sentence. The hallowed image that had been in my parents' minds was gone.

Mom was overcome with uncontrollable sobs, particularly when she heard about Angeline Diangello, the sister-in-law. Even Agent Vera was crying as she told of the husband dying in Angeline's arms. Dad was trying to comfort Mom but between her eruptions, Dad glared at me with a warning, "You'll be the next one crying."

Hearing Dad's warning, Agent Vera spoke directly to him, "Don't be hasty with Sebastian. He was an unwilling victim and performed better than any agent on our team. To date, we have been unable to incarcerate the Diangellos but it appears that they will end up behind bars because of Sebastian's integrity and contributions."

At that, Mom reached over and held my hand, "My hero."

"It's late. I need to be on my way. Please excuse me. Call me if there are any more surprises. You will be safe. We are monitoring the Diangellos' activity 24/7. Goodnight."

"Sebastian, it's a school night and late. We'll talk about this at another time," uttered my Dad. I vamoosed before Mom could say "wait."

I hit the sack and was out before thoughts of Dad's coming reprimand crossed my mind.

The next morning at breakfast, my eighth grade sister, Sarah, was blubbering about what to wear to a class county-court-house visit, scheduled in the afternoon. The teacher had promised that they would sit in on a trial in session and visit with the judge afterwards. My father's attempt to schedule "another time" was pushed aside. With Sarah saving me at the breakfast table, I was on my way to the bus before "another time" was scheduled. Other times when Dad would schedule "another time", he would back off if given a day to dwell on it. I counted on it happening this time.

As the school bus arrived at Emerald Ridge High School, all drive-in entrances were barricaded. The buses, dropping students, lined the inside lane of 184th Street East, a four lane east-west street in front of the school.

"Why clear out here?" I pondered.

Uniformed police were directing parents to drop off students almost a quarter of a mile away. With the entrances jammed with walking students, I was bobbing my head back and forth to find a way through the chaos of bitter, grumbling teens. The hiking students were fuming because they had to walk two extra blocks up a ramp to enter the building. Running against the flow, someone cold-cocked my chin and knocked me on my tail. A young person with no movement was lying on the ground next to me.

The dead were not a new mania to me. I had been at my grandfather's bedside when he expired while smoking a pipe. As the only one with him, I had to grasp his hand and wrench the pipe free to prevent burning the bedclothes, or maybe the entire hospital. That boy next to me, with a red welt on his temple, sure looked dead to me. Rolling over to be next to him, I put my ear to his mouth and felt a whiff of breath on my check. Rising to my knees, I systematically pressed on his chest as I had been taught in health class. Others gathered around to inquire what was going on.

"No, let me go. They have my sister and I'll be next!" he whispered as he awoke with a start. His squirming was like a cat when giving it a bath. My attempt to administer first aid was doing more harm than good.

I leaped to my feet, grabbed his arm and said, "Let's go. I know a place you'll be safe." Although he dragged his feet, I towed him to the carpentry class dumpster behind an annex shop. We raised the cover, leaned head first over the edge and found ourselves falling into a bin of wood shavings and sawdust. Lifting the lid slightly while standing on tip toes, I was able to thoroughly scrutinize the area and confirm our safe escape.

"We're okay. We'll wait a bit and then sneak out of here," I mumbled.

He wanted to see for himself so I let him step on my knee and peek out. With his face in the crease of light, I finally recognized him, Juan Espinoza. Homeland Security had hired me as a trainee to stand off at a distance, watch and report anything I could about him and his sister, Jel. His family's home had been bombed in Los Angeles and Homeland Security was collecting information on the whole family. To be with Juan in this way was an unexpected twist but I was glad I could help him.

He seemed comfortable after having a glimpse that all was going well. He lifted the dumpster cover another three inches to give more light and gave me a once over.

"You, oh no!" He fell off my knee, crawled to the darkest corner of the dumpster and moaned, "You're worse than a teacher or police. How did I get into this mess?"

In the short time that I had been at Emerald Ridge High School, I had sensed wariness from the other students. I hope I am humble, yet I am a person who others have to make an effort to know, so at the time I didn't really think about it. This was the first that I became aware that it might be fear. It must be the rumors of what happened in the last six months at Stahl Junior High School.

"Fill me in. I am one of the good guys. Why are you afraid of me?" I whispered.

The glaze that reflected from his eyes in the dim light told me that I might not get an answer. From the crack at the lid, enough light slipped in for me to see a two foot splintered two-by-four lying at my feet. Handing it to him, I said, "I'm not armed. You can use this if I get in your space."

Latching on with both hands, he swung it back and prepared for a go at me.

"Whoa, let's talk a bit first." The two by four was medicine that put him back in charge; some of his panic was gone.

"What have you heard about me?"

"Everybody knows you're that terror from Stahl. You organized a school strike, abducted a student and threatened to kill the vice-principal. Now you are in this enclosed dumpster menacing me."

"All that really happened but it wasn't me. I was only

indirectly involved. We don't have time to straighten this out now. To be safe, you keep that two-by-four handy until you change your mind." I didn't mind having a scary reputation. His willingness to respond to me was more likely if he was afraid of what I might do.

Without letting on that I recognized him, I asked, "What's going on?"

"Somebody put a cherry bomb in my sister's locker and it blasted as we were nearing school. My sister, Jel, and I walk and always come early. As we arrived, smoke was pouring from Jel's locker. Teachers, who were waiting for us, grabbed Jel before we knew they were after us. Instantly, I fell flat, crawled between the legs of a teacher trying to snare me and took off. You know the rest. I hope Jel is all right."

"She'll be okay. I have a friend who will take care of it. All we have to do is keep you out of sight until things stabilize. I'm Sebastian Boyle, a sophomore. Call me "SEBie."

"Yeah, I know. I'm Juan Espinoza, I'm a sophomore too." He was a good looking kid with a tan, and was well dressed. From earlier observations, I knew he was well mannered and it seemed out of character for him to assail me.

"I suspect the student body will be collected in the assembly hall for a couple of hours until a bomb squad can secure the school. It may be that the cherry bomb was a distraction to cover other activities.

"You remember the first day of school? That search-and-seize was because of a bomb threat. After the bomb in your sister's locker, the school will be in lock-down and the bomb squad will turn the building upside down before allowing school to start again. The scrubbing will likely take all morning, maybe all day if we are lucky. Nobody will be looking for us except for a couple of teachers."

I paused a moment to scheme. If I could get to a phone…then I had it.

"There's a phone in the annex behind us and the room is empty until an afternoon class. Juan, would you feel safe enough to stay here while I sneak in to make a phone call for re-enforcements? I'll be back in less than 10 minutes. Do you have a watch?"

"No."

His eyes still had the burst-from-within glare but a slight closing of his lids assured me that he was recovering.

"Here, take mine. If I'm not back in 30 minutes, try to find a way out." With him thinking I would return for the watch, I carefully lifted the lid, and saw no one. In a second, I was over the rim and on my way to the annex before he could say "no". Some one had forgotten to lock the annex door in the excitement and I was in.

"Agent Vera speaking."

"This is Sebastian. I'm phoning from the carpentry annex behind the school. Juan Espinoza and I are hiding in the dumpster in back of the annex. The school staff has Jel. Can you come out and straighten this out? I have to run. Thank you."

"I'll be right there and have the team check out Jel. Stay out of sight. 60 minutes."

Forgetting to be quiet and cautious, I charged out of the annex. As I whirred around the corner toward the dumpster, a custodian's truck was pulling in to park next to it. Waving my arms, I ran to the driver's window and shouted, "Don't park there, the dumpster may have a bomb! Wait until it can be checked. I was sent to warn you." With that, I skedaddled back to the front of the annex as if a tiger was on my tail. It worked. Wheels squealed as the driver backed and then spun the truck to clear the area. Leaping back to the dumpster, I flipped the lid open and yelled, "Let's get out of here. They'll be back within ten minutes."

Juan was only too eager. With his head springing up over the rim, he grabbed the edge and fell head first. I broke his fall and we headed across the ball fields into the forest. A four block path through brambles and woods led west to 122nd Avenue South, a four lane north-south street.

Emerald High School is out in the boondocks. After leaving the woods we were out in the open during our two mile walk along the street before reaching civilization. On 122nd Avenue South, several Sheriff Deputy squad cars passed us traveling toward the school but as each went by, we initiated a typical school-boy act for them. The drivers didn't even look our direction.

After the long hike, we entered the Chevron across from Fred Meyer at 176th and Meridian. I called Agent Vera and gave our location. Standing in the station and watching traffic, a sheriff's SUV, sirens whistling and lights flashing, wailed by as it departed from the school. When Juan saw Jel's red hat through the back window, he was certain that Jel was on her way to jail. Juan began to cry.

"But we haven't done anything. We weren't even around when it went off. Why are they blaming us?"

"No sweat. You'll be out of this in 20 minutes after my friend arrives." Then I shared with him about Agent Vera. Impressed with my description of my friend, the record of her experience in Iraq and her performance in the Seattle Homeland Security office, he absorbed my confidence that she would fix things.

Ten minutes later her black SUV appeared. I could tell that the Agent was elated to see us.

Juan was enthralled with her, even her scarred pink face and crazy hair style. She treated him as a younger brother just like she had warmly engaged me.

"Let's go get Jel," was all it took. On the way, the Agent called the home team and then updated Juan with,

"Jel's okay. The police are releasing her and she will be waiting for us at the police station. They tried to restrain the two of you to protect you. Since the cherry bomb was in her locker, everybody suspected that someone was after you two."

With a policeman at her side, Jel was watching from the front door of the station. Like a bulldog released from a cage after being teased with a cat just outside the screen, she tore to the SUV and was tugging on the door handle before the SUV stopped.

Letting the two have a moment, Agent Vera leaned close and mumbled in my ear, "The Diangellos stopped at the high school for 20 minutes after they left your place last night. The police don't know."

Raising her voice so the pair could hear, she said to me, "School will be closed until 1 P.M. Let's drop the Espinozas off and we can go over to the Chevron and get some lunch."

The Espinozas, holding hands, were nose to nose getting answers to "what-happened-to-you" and then turned to examine their rescuers. Sometimes words are not needed. Their expressions made it obvious that they thought Agent Vera and I walked on water.

"Are you two ready for school? Yes, Jel, I know who you are. I'm Homeland Security Agent Vera. I'm going to drop you off at school and be on my way. The restraint was only for your safety."

"Yeah, the policeman already told me," Jel responded.

Agent Vera dropped the Espinozas off on 184th in front of the school. They seemed pleased to be let out on the street, out of view of the other students.

Returning to the Chevron station, we picked up a pizza and root beers and ate in the SUV.

"After this morning, the rules have changed. I am lifting the "stay-away-just-watch" rule that I gave you earlier. From now on, you may be friends with the Espinoza pair which should give us more insight as to what is behind all this. Also, you should discretely quiz them if they know the Diangellos. After the Diangellos' stop at the high school last night, I'm certain that the Diangellos planted the bomb but there is no way to prove it.

"Why Jel's locker was selected is a mystery but we now know it was a distraction for an office break-in. A masked intruder carrying a black bag was purposely breaking in during the bomb scare. He didn't get in but successfully fled to the woods behind the school.

"Please contact me daily from now on. Here is a cell phone, 253 227-5963, all loaded with key numbers. Feel free to use it for personal use. Your home phone is #1 on the contact list; mine is #2 and Sheila's is #3," she said with a knowing smile."

I didn't want to carry a cell phone but accepted it without expressing thanks.

"I was just advised that the school has been cleared for afternoon classes starting at 1 P.M. so let's get you back." And she had us moving.

Back to class? After all this? Back to be being the central figure of Juan's rumor? This was Stahl all over again; and me, an innocent bystander, was pronounced guilty. Well, I had lived through it once and could do it again.

Blindsided by the morning's events, I was dawdling as I entered the Commons. Nothing-you-wanted-to-smell wafted in the air, mostly like burnt stale paper and dirty socks, reminding me of the Diangellos and what they had done. These guys weren't just after the money; they were part of a something more sinister. With a premonition of peril, I determined to take each day a step at a time. The first step would be to quiz the Espinozas.

All day, both teachers and students chatted about the morning's scare which shortened our class work. I was glad when the day finished and knew that I had escaped interrogation for my absence in the morning.

3 | *The Prank*

"Sebastian!" Bleary before my first class, I thought I heard my name but I wasn't sure. "Sebastian, stop." That was Sheila Comfort, my "almost" girlfriend. Almost? I had kissed her once but I had never asked her to be my girlfriend. Mom, a well mannered, highly ethical lady, had advised me that the proper way is for boys to ask girls and the girls can say no. I wanted to ask but was afraid that Sheila would say "no". Also, Mom had said,

"You talk to me before you ask any girl to be your girlfriend."

I wasn't about to talk to Mom so I didn't ask any girls.

I stopped and moved to the edge of the hall to greet Sheila. She immediately embraced me. Having Sheila as a friend was like having a tiger by the tail. She was, in my estimation, the prettiest girl in the school with her long blond hair, blue eyes and all body parts properly sized. But I never knew what was coming next. An embrace in public in the Commons, did I deserve this?

"Are you alright? Someone saw you and Juan Espinoza collide and fall. Then you disappeared. I looked for you in the auditorium. What's this on your chin? Are you hurt?"

What's with girls? Talk, talk talk. I was lost to the present world with her in my arms and wanted to remain undisturbed.

"SEBie can you hear me? Can you talk? Say something," Sheila said as she broke away.

"I'm okay, just a sore chin. I took Juan Espinoza to the nurse and we had to lay down for awhile. Hey, class is starting so we'd better hustle. See you."

After another study of my chin, we parted for class.

* * * * *

In a class later in the day, as the students settled, the door opened and an assistant principal, Ms. Webster, strode in swinging her arms briskly. A piece of paper was fluttering in her hand.

"Class, this is Assistant Principal Ms. Webster. She has an announcement," proclaimed Mrs. Trimbell, the English teacher.

"Before I start with the announcement, let me repeat the Emerald Ridge High student record policy. It is our intent that all students leave Emerald Ridge High School with good records. Bad entries are avoided if at all possible. Please feel free to share anything. It won't be put in your file. With that in mind, I will proceed with the purpose of this visit," voiced Ms. Webster as her hat wobbled with each word. She lifted the sheet.

Australian Shepherd Dog Show

Emerald Ridge High School Parking Lot

(Moved to Gymnasium if weather is bad)

Friday November 26, 2010.

Call for Reservations at 253 435-6300

$100 per entry

44335533667788

"Someone has posted flyers in storefront windows in Puyallup and Tacoma." She held it higher.

"This dog show at our school has not been authorized and Emerald Ridge High has no knowledge of who the sponsor is. We are being deluged with calls since 253 435-6300 is the school office phone number. In addition to local calls, parties in Bellingham, Portland and Enumclaw have insisted on registering. One call came from Vancouver, Canada asking for directions.

"This is a cruel far-reaching, costly prank, not only on the school but on those who make the effort to be here. Puyallup School District Security has agreed to have overtime personnel here to turn away the "walk-ins" who don't attempt to pre-register. Two Pierce County Sheriff Deputies will be on site in the event of trouble.

"The Puyallup Herald and Tacoma News Tribune are both printing quarter-page ads announcing that the show will not occur. The papers are providing this service at no cost to the school district. KIRO, KOMO, and KING are similarly providing "no-cost" support on their TV and radio stations in the school segments.

Glaring and propping herself on the teachers desk, Ms. Webster asked, "Does anyone have a question before I go on?"

Her stance was intimidating along with her appearance and behavior. She had a long nose, a long face, and a long neck. She wore hard heeled clod-hopper shoes, nibbled carrots at lunch, uttered snickers when saying "no" to students at the front counter, and was heard to whinny on the phone almost everyday. Rain or shine, inside or out, she constantly wore the same wide brimmed black hat with the brim turned down in the back. A three inch black ribbon, bowed in the back, added to its revulsion.

Ms. Webster and I had been together at Stahl Junior High so I was well acquainted with her. She didn't scare me anymore. But, she had something on someone in this room and was slowly presenting it. Two boys on the right side of the room were squirming as if they had failed to take a needed stop during the break. With another hat bob, she started on.

"I was hoping that someone would have a question. Are you all awake? "

Most nodded and were wide eyed with the story.

Finally a hand went up.

"Yes."

"Is this really happening?" a coy girl in a front seat asked.

"Yes, and the prank is by somebody in this room!"

With that, we all moved to the edge of our seats and were saying an unspoken "who". Each was scanning the others.

Ms. Webster raised her voice and said, "Yes, we know who but we just don't know why. So one of you was angry at the school and did this prank? Or was the purpose of this to be a distraction to cover another event?

"The cherry bomb scare this morning has everyone on edge: the police, staff, and students. At this point, the why for the cherry bomb is a mystery. We are all being extra watchful and all incidences are being examined in search of clues."

She didn't have to say that. We were all aware of the investigation inquiries. It was old hat. It was like asking "Did you plug it in?" when the TV didn't work.

"Fortunately in this case, the dog show flyer tells all." Ms. Webster held flyer again for all to see. "A number code at the bottom tells the time, date, printer and computer that generated the flyer."

She pointed at the number with her little finger.

"By analyzing the code, we know that it was made by an Emerald Ridge High computer and printer and by examining the log-on sheet, we know who made the flyer. It was created at 10 A.M. last Wednesday on the computer in this classroom." After saying this, she lifted her head and began eyeing each student.

Immediately a hand shot up. With his hand raised, Wiggly number 1 said, "I had the 10 A.M. slot but I didn't do it. A senior, at least he said he was a senior, bumped me off. He argued that seniors have computer bumping rights."

Ms. Webster wet her lips. "What's your name?"

"Jay."

"Can you identify him?"

"No. I haven't seen him around school and he looked as old as a teacher."

Whereupon, Ms. Webster demanded of Wiggly number 2, "Were you here to see this happen?"

"Yes. I was standing behind Jay while he was bent over the

computer so I had a better view. The guy had a stocking blue hat down over his ears and to his eyebrows. His eyebrows were long and into his eyes. He had ice-blue eyes. His collar was up higher than his chin. Not enough of his face was showing to be able to remember him. He was real tall, over six feet."

Students aren't supposed to be frightened at school when surrounded by over 130 staff members comprised of administrators, certified personnel, classified staff, and kitchen staff, plus 1600 students. But I was scared to death. I recognized this guy at once--Caterpillar Eyebrows. Brazenly he had walked into the school, interfered with a scheduled operation and used school equipment. Next he would strut into my classroom and tow me out by the ear.

In the dark about what really happened, Ms. Webster simply said, "You two, come with me and help us record this event."

Noting the time, Ms. Webster apologized for using all the class time and ushered the two boys out in front of her.

On break, I called Agent Vera. After I finished my account of the class events, she said, "Another distraction. I'd spend my last nickel betting the Diangellos are after something in the office safe. We'll have someone in the office the day of the called-off dog show.

"Don't be concerned. Our watchdogs reported seeing the tall Diangello go in and out of the school. They don't make a move that we don't see.

"Try to quiz the Espinozas today if you can. Call me after school. Don't forget. We've got your back." And the cell went to a buzz in my ear.

Failing to latch onto an Espinoza during class breaks, I stood at the long hall of locker panels after school thinking about the three mile walk home if I were to miss my bus. Ghostlike, Jel materialized at my shoulder.

"Something is going on. Juan is late and he has never been late. We hike cross-country through the undeveloped lot at the dead end of 184th Street in front of the school and a tan sedan is parked there. Two men are in it. I'm afraid to go by it."

"Let's find Juan first. I'll check the two bathrooms on this floor. It would be safer if you stood at the office door where you won't be alone. The office staff stays late. I'll meet you there."

Both restrooms were vacant and when I approached the office, the search ended. The principal, James Finn, was standing in his office, bending over the seated pair, Jel and Juan. My shadow at the office window caught his eye and he motioned me in. As I went in to his office I immediately focused on a banner

REMEMBER YESTERDAY
SURVIVE TODAY
LIVE FOR TOMORROW

hanging on the wall behind his desk. I agreed with SURVIVE

TODAY and LIVE FOR TOMORROW but there were things that I was determined to forget. The principal would probably say that I was keeping secrets.

"You three are keeping secrets and are hindering an investigation.

1. Jel--a cherry bomb was in your locker.
2. Juan and Sebastian--you were absent from school yesterday morning, and a pair with your description was seen at the corner Chevron during school hours. The Chevron doesn't want school lurkers and reports them.
3. The sheriff called to say that you, Jel, were released to Homeland Security and that you, Juan and Sebastian, arrived at the County Police station for Jel in the Homeland Security SUV.
4. Homeland Security immediately dropped you, Jel and Juan, at school after leaving the police station but you, Sebastian, were gone for another 30 minutes.

"Will one of you explain what is going on?"

Evident to any one who works with teens, the Espinozas had clammed up. It was apparent to me that Jel and Juan had not revealed details of our morning outing before I arrived. So, it was up to me to lie our way out of this. No, I wasn't going to start that again. My first inclination was to tell Principal Finn all; it couldn't hurt. But reviewing the directions that I had received from

Homeland Security, I realized that this was my first contact with Principal Finn and he was an unknown. I couldn't trust him. I, too, clammed up.

Principal Finn waited a full minute. "No volunteers?"

"This doesn't stop here. I'm going to contact your prior schools and review your records on file here. Sebastian, I've heard rumors of your theatrics at Stahl and know Principal Hugh Campbell well. I'll see what he has to say and then we'll have another session.

"Please give careful thought as to how you can help your school. I'll have the "after-hours activities" bus provide a ride home. The bus will be waiting at the Common's entrance. You're dismissed. Just a moment. Jel and Juan, please find a spot in the waiting room for a minute. Sebastian, we need to talk about one of your assignments.

Jel and Juan trudged out wondering if my lips would be loose.

"Sebastian, you are a top student; maybe the top. I can't believe that you won't share. Would you at least tell me where you were yesterday morning?"

"It's nothing really. After seeing smoke coming out of Jel's locker and then watching Jel be detained, Juan took off, ran into me out front and told me that "they" were after him. I grabbed him and vacated the campus until I could hear the rest of the story. I called Homeland Security Agent Vera, a close personal friend, to come and straighten it out. Juan and I met Agent Vera at the

Chevron station. Agent Vera made a detour to pick up Jel at the police station. From there, she brought the Espinozas back and Agent Vera and I went for lunch."

"Okay. Next time, please feel free to come to me, first, wherever I am. You don't need to call Homeland Security. You're dismissed."

"Right," I thought. "Walk voluntarily into his "we-know what-is-best-for-you" trap. No way. And something seemed out of place but I couldn't put my finger on it."

As I sauntered through the waiting room, thinking I may have said too much, Jel tightly grasp my arm and asked, "What did he want?"

"He cautioned me about using a wrong term. My Civics' teacher asked what my favorite holiday was and I said "Christmas." Principal Finn wants me to use "holiday" to avoid trouble for the school."

"Oh, I thought he wanted to know about yesterday."

As we walked through the Commons, Agent Vera's request flashed in my mind. This would be a good time to quiz them. "Wait a second. I want to give you a warning. Nobody is around but let's step over here to be sure."

They followed me to a corner behind a school news stand.

"Jel, do you recall the tan Hyundai that you saw out in the street?"

"Uh-uh."

"The Hyundai belongs to a pair of local brothers, the

Diangellos, who live in Devoreaux, three miles away. They are villains. Give them wide berth for your own safety."

These two Espinozas were like my dog when thunder and lightning cracks: Its tail goes between its legs, its ears droop, and it crawls under the bed. Their faces were ashen; they squatted behind the news stand and searched the Commons, every shady corner.

"Diangellos?" both whispered.

Not finding any menacing Diangellos, Juan was the first to recover his demeanor.

"The Diangellos are the ones who were after us in Los Angeles. We lived in an Italian community--we were unwanted second generation Spaniards from Barcelona. The Diangellos were the community's self appointed steering committee. But they were more like a mafia. Everybody had to bow or they were harassed with unfriendly visits. Dad owned a store and the Diangellos wanted a "business fee". After refusing to pay the weekly fee, Dad warned them and threatened to go to the police. The Diangellos were customers of the store and when they forgot to pay and walked out one day, Dad stopped by their house to collect. They were loading stolen furniture from their garage and Dad took pictures.

"Two days after Dad refused as I was strolling home from school, the Diangellos' stretch limo floated by like an aircraft carrier and docked in front of our house. Two men edged from the car, opened the trunk, lifted two black boxes with 2 foot cords hanging out and hunkered to hide the boxes. Stooped, they ran for the front of the house. Like a deer leaping a fence, I ran to the backyard, and to the back door screaming 'get out'! The family barely cleared the door as the house blew up.

"Our family followed Dad to our car and we left Los Angeles without looking back. We ended up here. Dad is well liked and had friends who found a security job for him at Pierce College."

Jel butted in and said, "Do you think they know we live here?"

I reached with both hands for her shoulders, put my nose a foot from hers, and locked my eyes with hers. Juan leaned in to hear and put his arm at my waist. "Both of you listen to me. Yes, they know you are here. But, you are safe. Stunts by the pair up here have caused authorities to monitor their every move."

Most of the gray debilitating residue in Jel's face washed away. Whereupon, she threw her arms about my neck and murmured in my ear,

"I love you. You are the best thing that ever came into my life. You're my hero," and held on as if she were a tourniquet stopping blood flow.

What's with girls; their power to control? When it became my turn to die, I wanted it to be like this as I was on my way to heaven. Sheila? Jel was two years older and I quickly sensed the difference. Plus it got even better. Juan was in back of Jel, wrapping us tightly to him. No, I had never had a girlfriend but I, at this moment, sure wanted one.

Someone was tapping on my shoulder. It was Principal Finn.

"The bus is waiting. You'd better be moving."

The three of us grabbed our back packs and boarded the bus. I put my finger to my lips, and we were silent all the way to our stops.

As I walked to the house, I tried the window to my room. It was locked. So I had to use the front door and expose myself to what was certain to come.

"What now? Where have you been? Why are you so late?" Mom was standing at the kitchen door with a bread knife in her hand. Homemade bread scents floated by me, enticing the neighbors' appetites. At that point I didn't care what she put me through. I wanted a slice of that bread with jam.

While she waited for me to close the door and cross to her, she said, "Last summer you promised to call."

She was still traumatized from the plight that occurred in our home with the Diangellos, the sheriff deputies, and Homeland Security two nights ago, and she was worried. This was going to be easy. She was on a high and would believe any tale I told.

"Principal Finn wanted to see me for a minute. One of the teachers is asking to start an off-hours reading club. The principal opposed it but wanted to check with a student before he said no. He asked me. I missed the bus and had to wait for the activities bus. I tried to call when I saw my regular bus was gone but the office was secured when I went back."

"What did you say about the reading club idea?"

"I didn't like it. I can't keep up with my homework reading assignments. Can I have a slice of bread?"

While eating the "best-on-the-block", I realized that I had done it again; lied. But it was justified. The story of my day would have taken an hour and then another grilling would occur when Dad came home.

4 | *Missing*

Burning the candle half the night, I caught up with two days of homework. I tossed my clothes on a chair, doused the light and was out before I hit the bed. Sleeping until the last second in the morning, I splashed cold water in my face to shake the cobwebs. Squirting toothpaste in my mouth to sweeten my breath, I swallowed it, and slapped on yesterday's clothes. Rushing by the kitchen, I jammed a slice of toasted homemade bread to take along. I hurdled through the front door, two-stepped the front steps and saw the bus starting to move.

Detecting my exiting tumble, the driver kept the door open and the flag out, and slowed as he eased in my direction. I soared onto the steps and said, "Thank you."

The driver cocked a thumb to the back as he pulled in the flag and shut the door. I didn't interpret his meaning so he said,

"If I miss you some day, you can hitch a ride with them. They follow me to the school almost every morning."

Out the back window I saw a tan Hyundai.

I retorted, "No way. Those guys are trouble. I'd run for my life."

Sure enough, the Hyundai followed the bus, patiently tolerating every stop the entire way to school. At the school, it proceeded straight past the bus turn-out to stop at the dead end of

184th Street East. Since Jel Espinoza had mentioned seeing them there one evening after school, it seemed that they were almost omnipresent. I grasped the benefit of having Homeland Security on their tail.

As I left the bus, Amin, my closest friend was waiting. Amin was a foreign transfer student from Iran and looked the part. He had kinky black hair covering his ears and drooping to his eyebrows. He wowed the girls with his smile and courteous attitude. While at Stahl Junior High, I discovered that although his American last name was Aflakian, his Iranian name was Bin Laden. Even with his undesirable family tie, a blood-brother relationship developed between us when we fought through several ordeals together.

Recently, here at Emerald Ridge, our paths had separated, him with sports and a science curriculum and me with a classic college curriculum. But the bond remained and we were together as opportunities were presented.

"Sheila said you hurt your chin. Are you surviving?"

"Thanks for asking. It hurts but I'm okay. Where were you when the firecracker went off yesterday?"

"On the bus. It went off before I arrived."

"Me, too. Hey, I want to do a little detective work. Want to help?"

A flicker bounced in his eye. "Really? How soon do we start?"

"Right away. What time do you leave after school? "

"I have to wait for a ride so I am around for 30-45 minutes."

"Find a place out of sight and watch lockers 343 and 123. Since they are so far apart, you will have to bounce back and forth to spot-check them. The lockers belong to Jel and Juan Espinoza respectively. Actually, 343 is Jel's new locker since she changed when the firecracker went off in hers. Inasmuch as they are friends of mine, I want to help. I need to know if anyone is messing with them. Be careful to avoid detection. We'll do it for a week. I'll fill you in with details when there is more time, maybe at lunch today.

"My cell number is 253 227-5963 and I have it on me all the time. You have a cell? No? That's okay. Drop a note in my locker, 154, if you detect anything."

I sensed his concern that there might be some risk so I thought I should clarify the risk.

"Police and school authorities have not found who put the firecracker in Jel's locker and they are still looking. You'll have to be careful to avoid being identified as an interested party. Are you game?"

"I'm in and will start tonight. I've got to go. See you." And Amin was aboard to help. By tomorrow, I'd know if the school was following up with investigations.

The morning classes were back to being boring: read this, memorize that, do these problems, and so forth. The only fun time was in the class with Sheila when she examined my chin and held my hand for two minutes. I wanted to ask her to be my girlfriend without having to talk to Mom but with Jel on the horizon, I waited. During a break after 3rd period, Juan snared me at my locker.

"The tan Hyundai drove into the student parking lot. Are they coming into the school?" Juan complained, wanting assurance.

"I couldn't guess what they are doing but I'm not worried. They are under surveillance. You could help if you jotted down when you see them. I have a log here in this pocket pad," and I showed him my log, a 3" x 4" spiral red pad. Having a task to fill my mind helped relieve my stress and I thought it might help him. I reached into my backpack and pulled out a spare pad.

"Thanks. Good plan; I'll tell Jel. See you." And he trotted off to 4th period class.

* * * * *

Amin and I shared lunch and sat at an isolated table by a window. As I told the Diangello story and about Agent Vera, he was ecstatic. Although he was not appointed to be on the Homeland Security team, having the opportunity to work with me thrilled him.

"It's like the 'A-Team' when we were at Stahl, only bigger and better. Thanks for asking me." Amin and I had been on an A-Team, partnered with the principal and a teacher, to ferret out several Stahl problems.

As Amin and I were dumping our trays, I saw Jel and

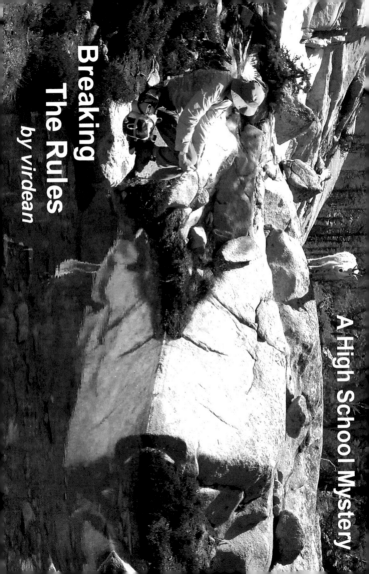

Breaking
The Rules
by virdean

A High School Mystery

From:

http://www.virdean.com -- "The home
of take along books that provide sheer
reading pleasure and unconventional
greeting cards that make a greeting
real."

wanted to introduce Amin. I put my hand on her shoulder and said,

"Hi, Jel. How you doing?"

She whirled around, shrugged off my hand and barked, "Keep your hand off of me."

It wasn't Jel but was the spitting image from the back.

"I'm sorry. Please forgive me. I mistook you for someone else. Is there anything that I can do to make you feel better?"

As I spoke, she fleetingly glanced down and said, "Oh my."

My eyes coiled down around her knees and then her skirt. Two red circles decorated her skirt. Observing her discarded tray, I saw a half-finished hamburger up on edge with ketchup oozing and dripping to the floor.

She filched four table napkins from the service stand and ran from the room.

Gazing at Amin, I asked, "Did I do that?"

"No, she did it when she laid down the tray just before she moved to escape your hand."

"Whew! Let's go to class."

I have sensors in the genes that I inherited from my grandpa. He could always tell when rain was coming. I could too, but my genes were stronger; they could tell when trouble was brewing. My subconscious was telling me that I had blown it big time and this was the start of something that would have repercussions.

The afternoon classes went fast. In American Studies, we

learned about eminent domain and how it had been applied to evict a Puyallup property owner to make room for the new city hall. In math, the challenges of new ways to use fractions were fun. I went home with my mind on my studies and homework, a normal day.

* * * * *

Each day was bringing its own thrills, good and bad. Finally caught up with my homework, I felt nothing could go wrong. On the ride to school the next morning, I noticed the Hyundai following the bus and smiled at their stupidity. Who intentionally follows a stopping school bus?

At school, hoping for a good day, I opened my locker. A folded note fell to my feet.

Three teachers are discretely watching lockers 343 and 123 from the end of the hall. Otherwise there is nothing moving, I mean nothing. Everyone is gone. The teachers work in 10 minute shifts and stand behind a corner as they watch.

A

Good for Amin. We'd stop the locker watch. Next, I would have him watch the Espinozas as they headed off for their hike after school. Since the Espinozas were the only ones who took the field route, anyone following would easily be detected. I slipped the new directions on a note into Amin's locker and went to class.

Instead of sitting at his desk and studying his lecture notes, Mr. Graves was standing at the door, motioning students to hurry to their seats.

"Please find you seats so we can commence. The buzzer has sounded," he ordered.

Before the last four were seated, he was holding a picture up and saying, "This is Lynn Whitney. Do any of you know her?"

About half the class raised their hands.

"Have any of you seen her today?"

No hands were raised. Mr. Graves sat and began taking notes.

"Did anyone see her yesterday afternoon?"

Several raised their hands. One spoke saying, "She is in two of my classes and she was absent."

More ventured similar comments.

Gloom had settled. Mr. Graves' disposition invaded the classroom and we were curious about why he was asking all the questions about Lynn. When he finally held the picture so I could see it, I recognized her as the girl who had left the cafeteria. Without thinking that I might have been the last to speak to her, I raised my hand.

"Yes, Sebastian."

"I saw her leave the cafeteria about 12:15 P.M. yesterday."

Two more hands flew into the air.

"Yes."

"Yeah, I saw her leave, too. She rushed out like she had to visit you-know-where."

"And you?"

"Me too. She was crying."

"Has anyone seen her since?" Mr. Graves asked as he wrote on the pad.

"No other sightings?

"Lynn didn't reach home last night and her parents have reported her missing. Attendance records show she hasn't been to class since 4th period yesterday. She has no close school friends here at Emerald High but her parents say she is close to several girls her own age in home-school. The home school friends haven't seen or heard from her either.

"We don't suspect foul play but we are taking precautions. Any information that you find or may have, please forward it to a teacher or to the office.

"Sebastian, would you take this note to the office? It merely records the results of the class survey. Thank you."

As I left the room, Mr. Graves was trying to draw attention away from Lynn. "I have a friend, a soldier who is serving in Afghanistan. Would you be interested to hear about what he has experienced since he recognized his civic duty and joined the Army to serve? "

As I departed, my mind was on facts about Lynn: her likeness to Jel, her rush from the cafeteria, her lack of Emerald Ridge friends, the Diangellos in the parking lot in the period before her disappearance, and my last words to her. Where could she go overnight without being seen?

The class was into the Civics lesson when I seated myself. I tuned in as the method of selecting federal judges was defined.

During the class breaks, we all talked of Lynn's disappearance without new information being revealed. I called Agent Vera and expressed my concern about the Diangellos being in the parking lot at the time of her disappearance. Vera put that one to rest. The Diangellos were merely turning around.

Proceeding to the bus as school ended, I carried my backpack at my hip for ease as I boarded the bus. As I was seated, a chocolate bar dropped out, fell into my lap and left a mark on my light trousers. Furious that wiping it with my handkerchief smeared it further, I swore. My Dad had sworn once when Sarah had spilled her milkshake in the car and I figured that I was entitled.

"Young Man! Out! Now! Swearing is not permitted on the bus." The driver was half-way to my seat to assist my exit as he shouted. Laughter followed me from the bus and I was facing a three mile walk home.

Without fanfare, I hoisted my pack and hiked at the edge of the street, hoping to catch a ride with someone. Within the first block, I spotted a napkin. With no reason to touch it, I went by but as I looked; I saw a red spot. Picking it up, I realized it had been one of the napkins that Lynn used to clean the ketchup. Then, there was another napkin, 40 paces further, and another a little further. Lynn had walked this way!

Clues come to those who keep their eyes open. I jogged for home, watching for more napkins. Gears were clanking in my head in rhythm with my jogging footfalls. Where could Lynn have gone, stayed overnight and found something to eat? The motive wasn't my concern.

Entering my street, I didn't believe what I saw. The bus was just departing my stop, its last stop. Reasoning about why, it made sense. I had started my trek almost immediately while the bus loaded for 12-15 minutes. Then the bus route took 30 minutes more--I could jog home in less than 45 minutes and beat the bus. Not bad! I'd better go out for track!

Exercise clears the mind. My path for the evening was clear. Lynn could only be one place. As I went in, I greeted my Mom,

"I'm writing a report on President Andrew Jackson and need to make a trip to the library. Can you run me over and I'll walk back?"

"Yes, if we go right now. You ready?"

Five minutes later, as she departed from the library for home, I said, "I'll grab a hamburger at DQ and be home by seven."

I entered the Pierce County Library checking all corners. Walking behind the fiction section, I spotted Lynn sitting and reading in a chair placed out of sight between two five-shelf open-face book cabinets. Placing my backpack on a table within her vision and digging into one of my books, I waited for her to acknowledge my presence. In a moment, I moved over and began scanning the shelves for a book, intentionally staying within her sight the whole time.

"Crap, what's with this place," I muttered barely above a whisper for her benefit and left for the front desk. I returned shortly and sat at the table searching through my books, looked around and saw her watching me. Flipping a few more pages, I shut the book, rose and approached her.

"Hi. Did you have to do a report on President Andrew Jackson? I can't find anything about his judgeship."

"Hello. No, I can't help you." Her eyes were open now but had been partially closed previously. Alert for clues, I saw her shoulders stooped and bent forward. She could barely sit up!

"What I need is a break. I've been chasing AJ for two days." I was back to my favorite game of nick-naming. "How about we drop over to the DQ? It's right next door; we can cross the lawn and be there in a shake. I'll buy—hamburger, soda, anything you want. I owe it to you after the cafeteria, yesterday."

As she started to say no, a drop of saliva drooped from the corner of her mouth.

Not wanting to hear "no", I said, "I'm SEBie. Tell you what. Let's leave our stuff here and make a quick trip."

Her eyes were saying "thank you" and she reached for her purse and jacket. "I'm Lynn."

Before we were done, she had absorbed two cheeseburgers, two fries and two peanut-butter parfaits.

"Lynn, remember I asked you what I could do to make you feel better when you left the cafeteria? The offer still stands. I can forget AJ for tonight if you want to talk. I'm a good listener."

"SEBie, you're really nice but…"

"My best quality is keeping secrets."

We were in the corner booth and had the place to ourselves.

"Well, I have to talk to somebody. Here goes.

"I have four older sisters so everything that I wear is a hand-me-down. As a result, my clothes don't survive and I am blamed. One Sunday, on the way to church my mother wasn't satisfied with the way I was dressed and decided to get a new skirt for me, my first ever."

Family problems? I didn't want to hear this.

"I knew that it would probably be my last new one and I was really picky. We shopped at three stores before I found one that suited me. It was expensive. Very expensive! Who cares? It was the first time anyone had spent a dime on my clothes.

"Dad was furious at the price and said, 'You've been tearing up all your clothes. If you soil this one, you'd better not come home.'

"On that day in the cafeteria, for one reason or another, all my clothes were in the wash and the only thing I had to wear was my new skirt. Then I ruined it with ketchup spots. I can't get them out. See!"

She stood and there were the spots, red as strawberry jam.

"You sure know how to pick out a skirt! I have a surefire

fix for that. Nobody will ever know about or see the spots. Where do you live?"

"On 88th Avenue East."

"That's close to where I live. After we leave the library, we can walk by my place and we'll doctor them with 'Outspot'. I had ketchup stains, four weeks old, on my dark blue suit trousers and you'd never know it. Want to try it?"

"Would you? You're a life saver."

"Where have you been for the last two days?"

"Here, at the library. But I ran out of money and was exhausted without something to eat. Thank you again."

"How'd you do that? The library is locked tight at night."

"It's simple, really. I spent every penny that I had at DQ about 6 P.M. last night and returned to the library. About 15 minutes before closing, I took my pack to the restroom, climbed to stand on a stool and waited until things were quiet. They check the stalls by looking under the door and missed me. I slept in a lay-back office chair and hid in the morning until it was safe to find a place to read."

"Were you going to hide for another day?"

"I didn't know what I could do since I couldn't go home and was out of cash."

"Let's go back to the library, pick up our gear and head out. Are you strong enough to walk home? I should warn you, your folks reacted and have everybody and his brother searching for you, even the police. I hope that we can make it without a side trip to the station."

She was already standing before I shut my verbose mouth. Arriving without detection at my home, I sneaked in for the Outspot. After the skirt was doctored, she was one happy girl. She threw her arms around me, cuddled me hard and then soft. Sheila? Jel? Lynn was just as nice and had the same effect.

"You're my hero." Hero? Mom's hero? Jel's hero? And now Lynn's hero? I wondered if I had that effect on all girls. No, never happen. My younger sister, Sarah, had certainly made that clear.

I walked with her to the end of her street and figured she'd be home by 7:30 P.M. The last thing I told her was, "Be sure to tell your Dad why you wouldn't come home." I'm a liar, not a gambler, but if I were a gambler, I'd bet all that I had that she wouldn't tell her father.

As I entered the house, now after 8 P.M., the family was into American Idol. I didn't stop but headed for my room to delve into my homework.

5 | *The Girls*

A note was in my locker the next morning. It was from Sheila.

> I need to see you. Meet me at the
> east end of the Commons during the
> first break.   *S*

I couldn't wait. The period moved like honey poured after it had been in the refrigerator overnight. I knew about cold honey because I had mistakenly placed a jar into the refrigerator and tried to put some on my toast the next morning.   Sarah blabbed to Mom and after a Mother-Son "chat", I wouldn't make that mistake again.

I was in the Commons two seconds after the bell rang. Lynn entered from the other side, caught sight of me, dashed to me, wrapped me in her arms, kissed me and said,

"I told my Dad. He cried and said he was sorry."

Then she kissed me again.

"You are the nicest man I ever met: my hero. I'm late and have to run."

She left me standing dumbfounded, not one of my parts

would move. There for a moment I had been in heaven again. Ten seconds later I discovered control of my members and lifted my gaze to see Sheila fifteen feet away, tears rolling like a leaky kitchen faucet.

I advanced to her and tried to put my arms about her. She wouldn't allow me to touch her.

"I thought I was your girlfriend." Bliss melted all my thoughts.

The last time I heard those words was back there at Stahl when we parted for the summer and she said,

"We're not boyfriend-girlfriend yet." And now she was staking a claim? I hadn't asked her and wouldn't have to. If I didn't ask her, I wouldn't have to talk to Mom.

Instantly, I threw my arms about her and forcibly kissed her. She didn't kiss back. I had some fence mending to do.

"Sheila, it wasn't like it looked. I don't even know her, although I know her name. Last night I did her a personal favor and she thought that I had saved her life. That was her way of thanking me."

"But you kissed her."

"I had to show her that there were no hard feelings. Uh... I kind of liked it."

Sheila moved in, circled me with her arms, and put her hands on my back. She leaned way back, stewed for 20 seconds staring into my eyes, and then put her chin on my shoulder.

"She was the one everyone was looking for yesterday. You

found her, didn't you?"

"I can't talk about it without violating personal and private family matters. We ought to drop it. Okay?"

"Well, Casanova, don't get to liking it too much. I have to be in the office in two minutes. I have news that I have to tell you. Meet me at the next break."

Thinking that I had managed to squeak through by the skin on my teeth, I journeyed to my next class, anticipating the next break. During class, I was only half-present.

"Sebastian."

Instantly alert, I responded, "Yes sir."

"Answer the question." The teacher, Mr. Burbank, was pointing at a problem scratched on the board.

"I'm sorry, I missed the question."

The class tittered and a football player snorted.

"What is the answer to this problem?"

$$y = (2x - x)/x + x/2 - 1 + x/2$$

I studied the problem for over a minute and processed it three times to be sure. I sensed it was a trick question, but then realized that it was not a trick. It was a question to see if a student grasped the elements of algebra.

$$"y = x"$$

"Correct." He shook his head back and forth several times and paused. "I don't know how you were able to provide an answer with your attention level today. But, correct. Any of you other students who didn't have an answer, don't feel bad. This is not an algebra class but this example introduces you to a class that is available to you when you become a senior. If you are interested, stop by and pick up the solution on my desk. Class dismissed."

I crashed to the Commons. Sheila was waiting and all was forgiven. She grasped my hands and expressed her concern.

"The principal and three assistants had a meeting yesterday. I was asked to take notes. Four junker cars have been parked in the student parking lot for over a month. Principal Finn wanted to identify the owners but couldn't. He concluded the meeting with, 'Parking is limited and I intend to prevent our lots from becoming junkyards. I'm selling all four for pickup by a junk dealer.'"

"After that, one of the assistants pointed out that non-students had been using the parking lot, specifically a tan Hyundai. Ms. Webster commented that it was a car that belonged to the Diangello brothers who had visited Stahl to find Sebastian Boyle."

Somehow, I end up being the fall guy every time but I didn't see how they could blame me if the Diangellos were using Emerald Ridge High parking lots.

"Principal Finn gave me the impression that he had a bone to pick with you.

"He said, 'We'll see. I'll have Sebastian come in on his first study hall.' I could tell that the interrogation will not be pleasant."

"Thanks for the tip, Sheila. I'll be on my best behavior."

"Let's have lunch together and you can tell me what he

wanted." Sheila was looking out for me and now wanted to be sure I would be alright. Analyzing how I felt, my feelings weren't love but knowing that she was there for me, I was real close to falling off that cliff. I hoped that I could repay her someday.

We parted, leaving me with another meeting on the agenda. Somehow, I managed to survive the next class without another blooper. As I left the class, a volunteer student office clerk handed me a slip.

Please come to the principal's office.

Ms. Webster

Taking my time, I dwelt on how much to tell. Thanks to Sheila, my thoughts were organized and now all I had to do was add the polish.

I greeted the office clerk at the counter with, "I'm Sebastian Boyle. I have an appointment with the principal."

"He's expecting you. Go right in."

No wait? Three others were in the waiting room before me. Did I jump the line? A pain jabbed my gut. My heart was high in my chest on the back of my tongue. Another pain struck, only this one was much deeper. I had gotten off easy last time after I'd been honest about where Jel, Juan and I had been that morning. I stumbled my way into the office.

"Sebastian, come on in. Shut the door, please."

The austerity, the cold and mechanical environment of the office and the superior attitude reflecting from his eyes made it clear that I could expect an undeniably unpleasant experience. I hoped that my "best" behavior would bear me through.

He was seated at his desk with papers and folders spread out, some with numbers: #1, #2, #3…

"Tell me about the Diangellos. Please, don't make me drag it out of you this time."

Talking as fast as the words would come, I gave him my prepared narrative.

"I met them once. They came to the house about 8 P.M. one night this fall, claiming to be Pierce County Police and were asking questions about a purse. While they were there, Pierce County Sheriff Deputies came and a little later Agent Vera. The deputies wanted to book them since they were impersonating an officer and carrying but Agent Vera let them go.

"Oh, yeah. Sheila Comfort told me that they came to Stahl's office last spring asking for me while she was volunteering. Ms. Webster dealt with them.

"Frankly, the way they look, they scare the life out me. I hope that I don't see them again.

"That's all I can tell you." A little of the truth will go a long way.

Three minutes passed as Principal Finn digested what I had said. He wasn't surprised at anything I said and I sensed that my information was not new. He must have a deputy friend at the station.

"Have you seen their car, a tan Hyundai?"

"Yes, it follows my bus in the morning, usually parks at the dead end of 184th but it pulled into the student parking lot once."

Again, he was not surprised.

After another long delay, he commented, "I'm not comfortable with those two around the school so often. Would you mind if I call your friend, Agent Vera, and ask her about them?"

"She'd be the perfect one to ask. I wish you would. Here's her cell."

"Thank you for your openness. You're dismissed. You are excused from class since there isn't time for you to rejoin it."

With perfect timing for beating the lunch rush at the cafeteria, I selected my standard, hamburger with fries, and occupied a table next to a window. Jel came in as the buzzer sounded.

Seeing me, she turned from the food line and approached me. I stood to greet her. Before I could emit one word, she had her arms about me and smooched me square on the lips. This was my day. I could never hope for another day to top this.

"SEBie, you did it again! I told my dad about the Diangellos living up here and…"

Sheila was heading my way with both guns blazing.

"He called Agent Vera. She assured him that the Diangellos were suspects and were being watched. Thank you!

You are my hero."

Hero again? I loved it.

Jel wanted one more and kissed me again before she left to get her lunch.

This time someone had turned on the showers and Sheila was acting the part of the sad clown at a circus. She had her hanky over her eyes but that didn't protect her blouse. It was stained from tears.

"Casanova, don't touch me. See if you can top the last tale."

Not being very far along with this girlfriend thing, I didn't know how to deal with it. I started to leave. But Sheila was really the "one" and I didn't want to lose her. I stopped and said,

"Yes, I have a tale. It's the truth if you want to hear it. Otherwise, I'm out of here."

"You do? You can explain a second time in the same day? Okay, I'm all ears. Just don't come near me."

I arranged a chair for her, offered half my hamburger and fries and she took them. Good sign.

"Remember when I was gone Monday morning? I was with Jel's brother, Juan. He told me how his family is involved in matters of National Security and they think I walk on water since I was able to make contact with Homeland Security. Jel was just saying thank you the way girls do. I don't know Jel or Juan, although I think of them as friends. Yes, I kissed her back; it was fun. Will you forgive me? I'll tell you about Principal Finn if you do."

At that, she swung her chair next to mine and held my hand.

"I'm sorry, I was jealous. Yes, I forgive you. What did Principal Finn want?"

I shared the tale that I told in the office. Sheila's face grew sterner as I continued.

"They were packing? Weren't you afraid? I would be!"

"Agent Vera says they are under 24/7 surveillance by authorities. I believe that to be true but Principal Finn will find out for sure when he calls Agent Vera. No, I'm not afraid."

The five minute warning buzzer burped so we broke for class.

At this point, I determined to avoid any more favors for girls although favors yielded unbelievable rewards. I spent the rest of the day steering clear of Jel and Lynn.

6 | *The Dog Show*

Two weeks after my office session, another invitation to the office arrived. Classes and school were operating smoothly except for the tan Hyundai which continued to follow the morning bus. Jel and Lynn were always friendly but cool on our occasional contact. Sheila must have bent their ear. Although I missed the "fun" get-togethers, deep down I was glad that I wouldn't have to face another tangle with Sheila.

As I arrived at the office, again it was, "He's expecting you. Go right in."

I entered without any idea what this was about, ready to eat humble pie.

"Sebastian, I've talked with Principal Hugh Campbell at Stahl and Agent Vera. Before I was able to reach Agent Vera, I contacted the Homeland Security office about her credibility. Her status and her service record are incredible. You have two valuable friends. I hope that I can become your friend too."

My genes weren't ready to say yes to that.

"I owe you an apology. Will you forgive me for being harsh and crude with you?"

"I thought you were fair with me but okay, I forgive you." He had no idea how much I had left out but I would take anything I could get.

"The reason that I asked you to come in is that I wanted to discuss the Diangellos. For some time, by stretching my thinking, I have surmised that there is a connection between the Espinozas and several abnormal occurrences in the school. I want you to be aware of these links because you are one of them. You will see that I have resources beyond those in the school district.

"I hope that you will be able to confirm some of these thoughts.

1. The Espinozas' house was bombed by the Diangellos in Los Angeles."

   Agent Vera told him? After a pause, I nodded.

2. The Diangellos that live here are related to the Diangellos in Los Angeles."

   I didn't know so I didn't nod.

3. The Espinozas deeply fear the Diangellos.

   I nodded but then wished I hadn't.

4. The Diangellos are being investigated by the FBI or Homeland Security."

   I nodded as I concluded that Agent Vera told him.

5. The Diangellos have been stalking you since January."
   I nodded. The bus driver would have reported the Hyundai trailing the bus daily.

6. The computer hacker that printed the dog show flyers fits the description of the tall Diangello."

   I let my gaze drift away as I thought about what it would mean if I nodded to this. Ms. Webster would have described the Diangellos. He was testing me.

"Another person has described the Diangellos. You won't be releasing new information if you nod. You would just be confirming the other testimony."

I nodded.

"Thank you for your honesty. I hope that you will come to trust me as you did Principal Campbell. I am not the police and am not restricted in what I say. I suspect there is a lot that you are keeping from me, especially since you are so close to Agent Vera."

I sensed an interrogation and that he was probing to find out how much I knew.

Principal Finn leaned close as if sharing a confidence.

"However, I want to be open with you in return.

"There was an office break-in attempt during the cherry bomb incident. The custodian who prevented the break-in described the assailant as extremely tall, maybe seven feet. I presume that he was the tall Diangello."

This was news to me. I wondered if Agent Vera knew.

"As I stated, I have concluded that the current series of problems here at Emerald Ridge are tied to the Diangellos. I have them in my radar and am taking steps to thwart their efforts to disrupt Emerald Ridge's security."

I began to like the principal. I began to believe that he was being open with me.

"The illicit dog show, which we suspect the Diangellos originated, is the day after Thanksgiving. Because of the school office break-in attempt, I assume that they want something in the school safe. We suspect the dog show is a distraction for another try at the safe. Agent Vera told me that you two talked about the need for office security during the dog show and she agreed to provide an agent.

"The fact is that there will be over 100 applicants for the dog show even though we've made every attempt to alert everyone. The crowd will be angry and lashing at the police and school security authorities. The disturbance along with barking dogs will serve as a major distraction."

I pictured the jam of motor homes, SUVs, and cars, each with a barking Australian Shepherd.

Principal Finn continued. "However, we must not be short sighted. It may be that the Diangellos intend to nab Jel or Juan or both at their home while we are focused at the dog show.

"For that Friday, would you, on the QT, invite Jel and Juan to visit you during the time of the dog show?"

"Let me call Mom." Lifting the cell from my pocket, I powered it and dialed.

"Boyle residence."

"Mom, it's Seb. Can I invite two friends over the day after Thanksgiving? One is a senior, Jel, and the other a sophomore, Juan."

"We'll look forward to having them eat the leftovers."

"Thanks, Mom. Bye."

"It's a go. I'll ask Jel and Juan this afternoon."

"Thank you, Sebastian. You're dismissed."

I caught Jel at lunch and extended the invitation. She used my cell to contact her Mom and had an immediate 'yes'. Later after checking with Juan, Jel said they'd be at my house by 8 A.M.

* * * * *

Thanksgiving arrived and leftovers filled the refrigerator. Turkey, dressing, two kinds of potatoes, four kinds of vegetables, buns, sweet rolls, and three kinds of pie were waiting for our after Thanksgiving party. Mom found a place in the freezer for the chocolate truffle cake, her favorite "sneak-treat".

On Friday, my ears were tuned for a car by 7:40 A.M. and I sprang through the front door to meet their car, a dark blue GMC SUV.

Juan rolled out moving about like a basket of puppies. Jel, on the away side, didn't let that stop her. Knocking Juan aside, she smothered me with a hug. Taking a breath, she said,

"Come meet my Dad."

Dad, who had folded himself from the car, grabbed my hand with both of his and pumped like he was drawing water.

"This is my Dad, Fernandez." His eyes were brown, his face as round as a coin, and he appeared to be about 45. He kept grasping my hand and pumping. I put my other hand on his to show I liked him too. On the last downward pump, he leaned to my ear and said,

"Words aren't strong enough." And then he relaxed back into the car. I slipped a piece of paper into his pocket while mentioning, "Here's my cell number if you need to contact Jel or Juan. We'll bring them home." And then I eased the door shut.

Jel's Mom, wanting a turn, had circled the car, and hugged me as soon as I was free. Hugged? I never had a hug like that. She hugged, then hugged and then hugged. She was an image of Jel but further developed. I soon was holding her tight, and tighter, and tighter. My emotions were finding a way into feelings--I must be growing up. At last, she kissed me on the cheek and whispered in my ear,

"I don't know you but I love every inch and pound of you. You are like a son." Releasing me, she strolled to the passenger side of the car, got in and they left without meeting my family. I didn't get her name.

Half the introductions were over. The three of us, arm in arm, stepped towards the house to finish the job. After viewing the warm greetings at the car from the front door, Mom and Dad were smiling and ready for company. Jel lifted her hand to Dad and said,

"I'm Jel. You must be Mr. Boyle. This is my brother, Juan." And then to Mom, "Thank you for having us. I'm good in the kitchen and I would like to help, if I may."

Mom wanted to get the chocolate torte cake back out when she heard that. "Sebastian, where did you find her?" she asked.

"Would you like some breakfast?" Mom invited. "No? Jel, join me and we'll go to the kitchen and make some hot chocolate." And she started for the kitchen.

"Mom, Dad, can we stop for a minute? I need to tell you something. Jel and Juan's home was bombed in Los Angeles by guys that may be related to the Diangellos. I asked them here today because I thought there might be a threat to them during a dog show at Emerald Ridge. Is that okay?"

Dad, being Dad, was ready with an answer. "We want you two to stay as long as you need to: a day, a week, a month, or whatever. We don't like the Diangellos either and have a score to settle with them, too."

Mom, sensing the deteriorating atmosphere, said, "Let's go, Jel." And she started to the kitchen again.

While learning about each other, the day went fast. Sarah soon joined Mom and Jel. In late afternoon, we kids were watching a rerun of NCIS when my cell beeped. It was for Jel.

Her eyes were on me as she talked.

"Dad surveyed the neighborhood and an empty tan Hyundai is parked, partly hidden by a hedge, two blocks from our house. Dad says not to walk outside when we come home."

"Jel, do you know what they are after?" I hoped that after the family day she would let down her guard.

"Sebastian, could we go somewhere private?"

I took her into the guest bathroom. I sat on the stool while she sat on the counter.

"Here's what happened. Dad had a store and kept accounts on a computer. Customers would charge their purchases on account and Dad would bill them once a month. It was a farm store that carried fertilizer and other items that could be used for making a homemade bomb. After seeing news of a homicide by a homemade bomb, Dad noticed a large purchase in his records. It was made by the Diangellos.

"Yes, the pictures of stolen furniture that Juan told you about were burning a hole in his pocket but this was murder and a lot bigger.

"The next time the buyer came, Dad asked him if he had a farm and what he was growing to use so much fertilizer. A day later, the Diangello goons came by and tried to impose a high weekly business fee. Dad refused.

"After they left, Dad copied the computer files, evidence of who bought the bomb material, onto a second hard disk and stored it under the spare tire in our car. After we found a home here, the disk was hidden behind a drawer in the kitchen but we were insecure after what happened in Los Angeles. So we asked the school to store it for awhile. It is marked 'Espinoza Family History' and is in the safe in the principal's office."

I thought about who had access to the school safe. Users would be the Principal and three assistant principals. The safe, enclosed in a cabinet behind the principal's desk, was bare except for a cash bag with money that students were collecting and lost-and-found items. The cash was a collection for a student who needed to replace clothes that had been destroyed by fire in her home. $50 wouldn't be enough to merit a break-in. To me, this confirmed that the attempted office break-in was for the disk!

Right there I dotted an *i* and crossed a *t*. Someone, an insider, had tipped off the Diangellos.

Watching Jel's eyes wander like a strobe, I realized that she was not telling me the whole story. Her eyes were shifty and were having trouble staying focused on anything for more than a second. I supposed the school safe was a ploy. The original hard disk was probably in an associate's bank vault.

I imagined the Diangellos' anger if they were eventually successful in acquiring the hard disk from the school safe, only to discover it to be a fake. Recalling how they behaved when they visited my house, I anticipated that they would raid the Espinozas' with guns out and take Fernandez captive.

"Jel, these guys are desperate. I think Agent Vera should be advised."

"No, we can't do that. Dad was doing business on the side and avoided paying Los Angeles B & O taxes and IRS taxes. He'd be thrown in prison if authorities had the hard disk."

"Will you think about it and ask your dad? Homeland Security wants to incarcerate the Diangellos so badly that they would grant clemency for almost anything short of murder. Let's go see what happened to Gibbs". Gibbs was the main character on NCIS.

The Boyles day ended on a high. We drove the pair right to their door and Jel and Juan expressed their thanks for the best day of their lives.

Later, on a call to Agent Vera, she said that nothing had

happened except the Diangellos spent the day on foot. They split and watched the front and back doors of the Espinozas' house and wandered around their neighborhood. I told her that according to Jel, the Diangellos are after something in the school safe and I believed that they would kill to get it.

This Diangello rut was growing deeper each day. It was like seeing popcorn kernels floating in simmering grease ready to explode any second. I hoped that Jel's dad would turn in the disk and put the fire out.

7 | *The Soldier*

I was anxious to see Jel on Monday. Would her Dad agree to ask for clemency and release the disk? My mood was first-class after four days without studies. With spirits high, I was ready for anything that came my way. I wasn't going to let anything bother me today, even if Fernandez's answer was no.

Intercepting Jel before the first class, I asked,

"What's the word?"

"My Dad wants to wait."

And wait we did. As December passed, the persistent tan Hyundai fulfilled my expectations; it was there. But quiet reigned on all other fronts. Principal Finn made sure that he greeted Jel, Juan, and I each day. I assumed it was his way of keeping tabs on those who were most susceptible to attack.

The last day before winter break, I crossed the threshold to my Civics class with homework all done and betting that none would be assigned. A soldier in full parade dress was at Mr. Graves' desk. Was this what I hoped it would be?

Animated, a proud, glowing Mr. Graves stood with his visitor and motioned for the students' attention.

"This is my close friend, U. S. Army Staff Sergeant John Newton, currently back from the front in Afghanistan. I have asked him to talk to you as a highlight for your winter break. But before I do, I want to inform you of his thoroughbred pedigree. He won't tell you, but he has an ancestor who was a crewman on the Mayflower as it brought early American settlers across the Atlantic in that severe winter. If some of you are history buffs, you can see a replica of the Mayflower in Boston. Well, here he is. Please welcome him."

Mr. Graves never failed to inject plugs of American heritage and thus spoiled any applause there might have been.

"Hi Class. I am not a teacher, politician, preacher or a speaker. This is my first attempt to speak. I need your help as I share. I will ask questions as I go along. Any answer that you give will be right! There are no wrong answers today! Please, don't try to be funny but if that's all that you have, it's okay. I need to hear from you to see if I am on the right track. Nod to me if you agree to these rules."

Most nodded.

He walked back three seats along the wall row.

"Please stand and step away," he directed the student.

The seated girl stood and stepped away. He seated himself, stretched his long legs into the aisle and said. "Ah, I'm home."

We all thought that he was going to speak from there but after 30 seconds he stood, yielded the seat and courteously thanked the girl.

As he filed to the front, he said, "Everyone, please stand. Good. You're in the Army now for the next hour. Soldiers, you have just submitted to an order and are hereby sworn in. You may be seated."

Even Mr. Graves, who had rolled his desk chair aside, had followed suit.

"Now, we are going to learn Army talk. HooRah. What does that mean? In the Army, if you understand an order, if you agree, if you like something or need to respond to most anything else, that's the word you use. Nobody knows where HooRah came from. Let's try it. When I hold my hands down here like this, you say 'Hoo' and when I raise them to point at you, say 'Rah'."

He put his hands down and there was a squeak as the class responded.

"I'm disappointed. You'd never make it through boot.

"I sat in class as a sophomore just like you. As a matter of fact, I sat in that seat," and he pointed to the seat he had borrowed from the girl, "for a year listening to Mr. Graves at Puyallup High School. That was before Emerald Ridge was built. Mr. Graves taught me love for my country, to think and make decisions.

"Those lessons have saved my life, twice."

The soldier did a right face and saluted Mr. Graves.

"Thank you. I wouldn't be here if I hadn't listened to you."

Mr. Graves reached for his handkerchief and wiped tears from his eyes. "You're welcome. I know you never talk about those times and I do not intend to force you to do it today. Please continue."

The soldier did an about face and pointed to Old Glory in the corner. "With that here, I know I can do this."

He did a right face to face the class. "As I said, I'm going to test you at times to see if you are learning your lessons. Today, you will have to think and make decisions."

He put his hands down. Another squeak. "You can't even enlist if you can't do better. We are going to practice. Ready? Wait. Mr. Graves, I want you to stand here in the center and put your finger to your lips and rotate your head back and forth; like this." And he demonstrated what he wanted.

"Soldiers, Mr. Graves is giving an order for you to be quiet.

"I'm going to be over here and give the HooRah sign. Here's the deal. Teachers are prohibited from disturbing other classes. If they do, they are suspended. On the other hand, I'm going to ask you to do something that will cause Mr. Graves to be suspended. If you want to protect Mr. Graves' job, follow his command.

"Graves, you're in the Army now. Last names only. You know what you have to do to keep your job. Here goes."

The Sergeant lowered his hands. The class erupted "Hoo". One girl kept her lips sealed. Then the sergeant raised his hands. "Rah." The girl joined the melee. Not seeing one silent student, Mr. Graves moved to his chair and sat mutely.

"You all have now been promoted from boot to private. That was great. And, Private, I saw you think and make a decision," he said as he pointed to the girl who missed the "Hoo".

"One more time before I start my talk." His hands moved down and then up within a half second. "HooRah!" rocked the walls. A fluorescent lamp shade fell and a number of books fell from desks.

"That's the best HooRah I've ever heard. The timing and volume were perfect. You are all promoted to corporal."

He reached for three pages of paper on Graves' desk, read down the top page for five seconds, looked up, and said,

"After hearing your HooRah, I want someone to make a decision. These are talk notes about the Army and why you should consider it as a career field."

He waved the three pages over his head, dropping one.

Pointing at his forehead, he continued, "In here, I have true stories about four people who live in your community. I'm certain that all of you will know at least one of them. Which topic shall I talk about?"

He fluttered the paper with his left hand and pointed to the side of his head with the other.

"One of you is going to decide." With that, he picked up a marker pen from the desk, walked to a boy in the back seat, tapped the top of his head with the pen and asked,

"Corporal, what's in there? Can you make a decision?"

"Yee-e-es, sir."

"Do you need time to think?"

"Yes, sir."

"Class, he needs facts to help him decide. On my mark, I want all of you to vote. Here are some facts that may affect your vote. These are war stories; none are pleasant; you will not read about them in the paper nor see them on TV. If you want to hear the stories, shout 'HooRah' on my first command; if you want to hear the pep talk to enlist, shout 'no' on my second command."

He lifted the pen, held it for a second and then dropped it.

The HooRah blasted forth as before but louder and longer. There was not one "no" when he repeated the gesture.

"What's your decision, Corporal? No, don't bother. You gave me your decision. I heard your HooRah."

"Okay, stories it is. These are true stories. I may have to stop from time to time to control my emotions. Time is limited and I ask that there be no questions."

The door banged open and Principal Finn exploded in like when a firecracker detonates under a tin can. Smack! The door hit the wall and rebounded into his face. Shielding himself with his shoulder, he shouted "What's the racket?" and then he saw the sergeant. Swallowing his malice, he shut the door and quietly cleared a table for a seat.

Hearing the principal, the soldier remained at attention, waited for quiet and then began speaking,

"Out of courtesy for those involved, I am not allowed to tell you how I heard these stories but they are not gossip.

"A lady lives less than a mile from here, out east on 'view' ridge. Her husband, Tony, a soldier, was captured and held in an Afghanistan prison. After about 14 months, he was released and the Army flew him back to Andrews Air Force Base in Maryland. Let me divert for a minute.

"Andrews Air Force Base was named after Lt. General Frank M. Andrews, the highest ranking officer to die in combat at the time of his death. He was killed in Iceland."

My mind clasped a new thought. "It might be exciting to be in the Air Force and fly around the world."

"Back to the story.

"On the flight back, the 747 was full and Tony was the last off. A step ramp, like you see in the news on TV when the president uses Air Force One, was employed to offload passengers. Tony's wife, our lady, recognized him by the nod of his head as he weakly writhed and swayed his way down the long flight of steps, grasping side rails and stopping on each step to keep from falling. He had a long grey beard, his hair was white, and he was thin as a rail. As he let go of the stair hand rails and braved his first step without support onto the tarmac, a jitney pulling four luggage carts was accelerating and the fourth cart broke free. The heavily loaded cart smashed the returning prisoner as a dump truck would a pedestrian. His wife crashed though the retaining barrier and ran to him but in a few moments, he died saying 'goodbye' in her arms.

"What would the woman decide if she was asked to serve her country? 'Yes' or 'I've given enough?'"

The sergeant walked to the center of the class, bent over to whisper in a sniveling girl's ear. "What would you say if you were that woman?"

The snivels grew to be a wrenching sob.

"Do you know the lady?"

She shook her head no.

"Make a decision. Yes, no, or I don't know."

Frustrated and angry, she shot to her feet and screamed in his face, "I don't know."

The sergeant straightened, winked at Graves and returned to the front of the class. As he went, he asked, "Is there anyone at all who is willing to vote?"

He let his eyes drift about the room. No one volunteered.

"You, who are from Stahl Junior High, know Principal Hugh Campbell and that he holds an Olympic Gold Medal and was a marine that served in battle in Iraq. But here is something that he didn't tell you. He has a Purple Heart. Yes, he was shot! Medics thought his life was over but after four operations and three months in the hospital, he fully recovered. After his hospital stay, the army wanted to give him an honorable discharge and fly him home. Yes, he was discharged! I have two questions. The first, what do you think he did? The second, what would you do?"

The sergeant wandered to the back of the room. The students wouldn't look at him. He marched up and down two rows, head high and shoulders back. From there, he went to face Graves.

"What did he do?"

"I'd bet money that he refused the discharge, tore up the flight tickets and stayed to fight."

"What would you do?"

"I'd do the same thing!"

"HooRah!" bounced off the walls again.

"I knew that would be your answer. That's why I asked you. HooRah!"

"Graves, I've two more stories. Time is running out. Can the students stay over?"

"I'll answer that," Principal Fin interrupted. "If any student wants to stay, you can tell your next teacher that you were with me. I'll have signed passes on the office counter if you need them for your teacher."

The buzzer announced the end of the class.

"I need a break. Corporals, if you want to or need to leave, you may. I am not used to talking to so many and the fewer the better. I'll see you after the break," and he made his way out.

While the students filed out, a HooRah started and it was another blast. Pumped up as I had never been, I couldn't wait until I was 18 and could enlist.

It was the shortest break in history. Students were in their seats early. All returned. Students from the next class walked in, saw their seats taken and settled to the floor in the aisles. After hearing the HooRahs, others had come in and joined the class. Every space was filled with a body. Two lines deep stood along the walls, two across were seated in the aisles and 30 stood around the teacher's desk in the front. The door was left open for another 40 to 50 in the hall.

Principal Finn announced to the newcomers that if there

was a question about their absence in another class that they should say that they were with him or pick up a signed pass at the office counter.

"Mr. Graves, please proceed," he ordered.

Graves proceeded.

"Newcomers, this is U.S. Staff Sergeant John Newton, just returned from the front in Afghanistan. You can get the details of the first hour from the 'Corporals' that were here."

"Please continue, Sergeant."

"Does anyone have a question?" His head turned methodically as he eyed every student where each sat or stood. His uniform and posture were ominous and no student was brave enough to speak up.

After a pause, a girl four seats back meekly raised her hand 12 inches above her desk and then lowered it. To see her make such a motion stunned me. She was normally quiet, timid and stooped to avoid anyone's attention. When the teacher addressed her with a question, sometimes she cried even though she could give the correct answer. She never raised her hand even for special credit. One time she didn't give the right answer and ran from the room when another student provided it. To see the temporary hand motion indicated to me that the drive of this heroic soldier was seeping into the girl and she had made her first brave move.

Graves had requested that PA equipment be brought in. It had arrived and he stopped the sergeant to fasten a collar mike. Two speakers were placed on Graves' desk and one in the hall.

"Thanks, now I can speak without shouting like a sergeant," he spoke into the mike, grinning. Using the sound of the sergeant's voice as the test, a student adjusted the volume...

"You're welcome," the speakers blurted as Graves responded. When the sergeant glanced at the system, he realized that it was top-of-the-line portable PA equipment. All of the words he spoke as well as anyone speaking close by would be amplified and recorded.

"HooRah," he murmured as a first word on the recording.

"Okay, Corporal, sorry for the interruption, I'll come for your question."

He side-stepped and stumbled his way over the clutter of students in the aisle. Two girls, squatted on the floor next to the shy girl, stood to make room. The soldier dropped to his knees, placed his arm across the desk behind the girls shoulders asked, "What is your name?"

"C-C-Carol."

"Corporal Carol, Do you have a question?"

She shook her head. But with him so close, she could see her father's warmth. She sensed that this strong uniformed soldier had a wish to hold her and comfort her.

"Uh...yes. Mr. Graves said that you didn't have to tell about some of your experiences. Would you come back sometime and tell those stories too?"

The sergeant placed his hands on the side of her head, palms over her ears, and softly caressed her hair with his fingers.

It was as if he were trying to say "no" to his daughter. In a few seconds his handsome rugged stern face began to melt, his eyes blinked shut, and corners of his mouth coasted down. He bowed his head so no one could see for 20 seconds. Raising his face, composed, he said,

"I'm sorry. I'm not strong enough yet. Will you forgive me if I say no?"

Exposed to his face, she saw that just the admission hurt him deeply, whereupon she began weeping. She reached towards his face, fondled his cheeks, and said,

"Yes."

He tripped his way to the front and stood at attention to collect his thoughts.

Graves leaped to his side and said, "Sorry, I didn't plan that." Digesting what had happened and how weak the sergeant must appear to be to the students, Graves went on. "Sergeant Newton is probably the bravest man that you will ever see or hear about. Recently, I visited a friend in the Pentagon and was able to peruse Sergeant Newton's jacket, his military file. Sergeant John doesn't know that I did but I'm going tell you some of what was recorded there.

He pointed to a medal on the sergeant's chest.

"This a Congressional Medal of Honor, the highest medal awarded. It is granted for extreme bravery. Maybe one in a million has one. He has two. See this? It is a Purple Heart. He was wounded three times! On his back from his neck to his hip is a scar from a mine blast. Here on his right side, front and back, are scars where a bullet passed clear through. Down here on his thigh are similar scars where another bullet ventured through. Each injury forced three to four weeks of hospitalization and, for each; the army offered an honorable discharge, a return home and full benefits for the rest of his life.

"I won't take your time describing these other medals," he said as his hand brushed across them. "But I can't stop until you know one more thing," he continued as he pointed to a Combat Bronze Medal.

The sergeant was in shock that anyone had discovered all this. He was trying to interrupt but Graves raised his voice and overrode him.

"He was a prisoner of war for nine weeks. He escaped and in the process brought his Humvee crew, three other guys, and a second crew of four back to safety through more than 50 miles of enemy habituated territory

"Shut your d... mouth. You're making my talk-job harder." The sergeant was furious. Red streaks were creeping up his neck.

"One more word and I walk out," and the soldier stepped toward the door.

Graves had finished and went to his seat.

The sergeant was at a loss for words. He turned to Old Glory, saluted and then said,

"Corporals, please stand and give the pledge."

As one, they stood and repeated the oath with their right

hands respectively over their hearts. "I pledge allegiance to the flag…"

The sergeant joined them and afterwards said,

"Your devotion makes me feel better. Graves didn't tell the whole story. I am not a knight in shining armor. I was diagnosed insane and spent nine weeks in a mental institution. After the escape from prison, I lost it. Prisoners were severely abused. Yes, me too. And as a result, I viewed my keepers as a rat infested nest. I wanted to exterminate them: man, woman, and child along with their dog, cat or any other pet they had. A Catholic Chaplain, I'm not Catholic, seared through my fog and helped me see that if I did those things, I was a tool of the devil and no better than my enemy. Subsequently, after many tests and evaluations, I was released and diagnosed to be of sound mind and body. However, the prison experience changed my goals. I no longer wanted to be a medic. I became a fighting soldier.

He looked healthy and great to me. I am sure that others saw him that way too.

"I'm certain that one or two of you are wondering what I am doing stateside. Why aren't I over there fighting?

"My mother has a terminal illness and this is the last Christmas that I can be with her. The U.S. Army had a heart and ferried me back.

"I see two of you crying. It may be that you have a similar dilemma. I hope if I share my experience, it will give you insight to what you may be facing or maybe give you relief in your grief."

I could feel his grief as he spoke even though I didn't have a similar dilemma.

"She is in Good Samaritan Hospital on life support and this is probably her last lucid day. She is undergoing treatment until 1 P.M. and I hope to be at her side by that time.

"There is no hope. She is in extreme pain and has insisted to be relieved, that is, let her die. Without life support, she would only last a few seconds. With life support, her failing heart will give out very soon. The doctors are saying the big day is the day after tomorrow.

"Big day? She has been a saint all her life and I'm sure that there is a hallowed seat reserved for her at the feet of the Supreme King. The day of her heavenly reward will be a big day."

I felt the same way about my saintly mom and although she showed no signs of illness, these words were an encouragement to me.

"Upon completion of the funeral, there will be a Humvee waiting to ferry me to McCord Air Force Base to catch a C17 Globemaster III flight for the east coast and from there to Afghanistan.

"Let's get back to the stories. I don't know what you must think of me now that my insanity is no longer a secret. Can I get a vote to hear the remaining two?

"HooRah!" With the added voices, I was sure that we could be heard as far away as the Chevron. I was thanking a higher authority that I was in this class and could participate.

Something was bothering the sergeant. He concentrated for over a minute and then said,

"Corporal Carol asked me to do something that I couldn't do. But she needs an answer. I have an alternate answer.

"As fellow soldiers, we have to be straight with each other. In battle, you can't afford to play politically correct word games; you speak your mind and tell it as it is. I will do so now.

"I am not a politician so I don't have the ability to charm an Eskimo out of his parka and sled team in the middle of a blizzard. I am not trying to charm you now. But, how to deal with life and death experiences was not taught to me in school so I will give you your first lesson."

With that, the sergeant made eye contact with every soul in his sight. Several minutes went by as he made up a real life story that a student our age could relate too.

"You are in your front yard working with a pry bar to move a rock in a flower bed as a car approaches. A dog whips across the street and the car dodges. The tires squeal in protest but the car rolls 360 degrees. The driver, a man, manages to break open the damaged door and climb from the vehicle. He reaches back for a passenger. The man and woman crawl out to safety and the man collapses, injured, to the ground. Trauma seekers surround the car and gawk for movement in the completely lifeless injured man. Within seconds, a policeman arrives and pushes people back. The woman passenger is screaming, "My baby! My baby!"

"Flames begin to spike from the crack around the hood and

embark along a fractured gas line on the grease-coated underside toward the gas tank."

"It's a mad house. The policeman is shouting, 'Stay back, it's going to blow!'

"And the mother is screaming, 'My baby! My baby!'

"At that point, you hear a wail from within the car and see motion of small arms, and then a head through the back window."

"You observe the frozen state of all those viewing the scene. What do you do?"

The sergeant again stopped and scanned almost every eye. When he caught mine, I leaped to my feet and yelled,

"Run to the car and try the door. If locked, jam the pry bar into the crack next to the door handle to break the lock and open the door, reach in, release the car seat and drag the baby out. Then, run like h…"

The sergeant bellowed, "HooRah!"

"And that's the way it is. There are a few seconds where you expect the end, and then it is over, one way or the other."

"If a crisis like that happens more than once, a rumor goes around that you have a 'death-wish.' In the Army, when the commander hears the rumor, you are scheduled for psych exams. Those exams, rehashing those ordeals, are worse than living the ordeals. It's like you guys when you are caught cheating on an exam and what the teacher might do gnaws on you all day. The psych exams gnaw at every fiber in your body.

"I hoped that this example was enough to answer your

questions about what it is like. You just do what needs to be done. You're not a hero, just a soldier doing his job, a job that you can't talk about."

The room was silent and motionless as each of us tried to picture ourselves in that situation.

"Some of you may be thinking, there are two sides to the story. You only told the good side."

The sergeant hesitated as if he was searching for words. Then he said,

"Okay, here is the bad side. In the army, we sometimes joke about an easy way out. Is the term 'short-timer' familiar to you? For you that haven't heard the term, it is a term the army uses to define someone who will be discharged in a few weeks.

"As a short-timer is preparing for the discharge, he or she must 'muster-out'. That is, return equipment in his charge, his rifle, ammunition and other items. Almost every time, something is missing and forms must be completed to explain why. Also, a short timer must clear outstanding items in his personnel records. With the paperwork involved, it's irritating leg work, standing in line and a dreadful nuisance. Paperwork is full of errors, not of your making. Each error must be dealt with meticulously and cleared. We all feel that to "muster-out" is like "death-warmed-over". We can always tell who is a short-timer. They go around with a scowl on their face and swear at anyone they meet.

"I'll tell you a secret. If something should happen in that moment of bravery, you are a short timer who doesn't have to muster out. HooRah!"

A commotion at the door drew my attention away from the sergeant. Agent Vera? Here? She had squeezed through the throng to stand in the back row at the door. At her feet, on the floor, were Jel and Juan.

Crawling on her hands and knees, Sheila bumped her way through and wasn't letting anything stop her. The fireball wormed her way to my desk and sat on it, blocking my view.

"Okay to start the next story?"

Like one voice, the students shouted, "HooRah!"

The sergeant, encouraged by the HooRah, began the third story.

"A woman, who drives a black SUV and who you see here on campus occasionally, was serving the last day of her enlistment in Iraq when a Taliban insurgence threatened a critical supply line. A war-worn master-sergeant recognized the threat and asked for volunteers. This woman insisted she should be on the team to go. The master-sergeant refused but relented when she informed him that as she was the only one versed in the Iraq language, she was the best qualified. She would be needed if they were caught.

"The team was successful in thwarting the Taliban thrust but on the way back, their Humvee struck a land mine and was wiped out. Three of the crew were annihilated. One was found breathing, this woman. Medics stabilized her and they flew her back to Walter Reed Hospital in DC where proper specialized care could be administered. For a week, it was touch and go. One morning, an eye blinked and the staff knew that she had turned the corner. Broken bones, torn ligaments, severe lacerations--I can't begin to list her traumatic conditions. She was not a quitter. Fourteen months later she walked out of Walter Reed on her own without crutches or a cane."

"HooRah!" shouted the students.

"Wait, there is more. Her entire face and scalp were blown away by the explosion. Her face, scalp and hair were replaced. It was a miracle. Would some of you like to have a new face or a different head of hair?

"What did she want to do? Stay home for an easy life or go back and fight? I need a girl this time. Is the Captain of the basketball team here? Is that you?"

The soldier lurched and slipped through the bodies to a tall brunette standing in the back line of the room.

"Do you need some time to think?"

"No sir."

"Do you need more facts?"

"No sir."

"What is your decision?"

"She'd want to fight."

"HooRah! What would you want?"

"The same as her."

"Join me in a HooRah for this fighter."

"HooRah!"

Standing with the girl, he said, "The rest of the story is not what you would expect. Doctors told her that her injuries prevented her from regaining 100 percent of her strength and that she was being discharged. She could not go back. She competed for a Homeland Security position in the Seattle Office. I am proud to say she has been awarded the Office Top-Agent award for the last two years."

As he was speaking, he was working his way back to the front. When he stepped to the clear area behind Graves' desk, he glanced to see the size of the crowd in the hall.

The Agent bowed her head to avoid detection. The Sergeant recognized the tufts of hair over her ears and immediately made his way to her.

"Please forgive me. I didn't know."

"It's only a drop in the bucket. Don't worry about it."

"Will you give me the honor to present you to the class?

"They'll recognize me anyway. Sure."

Solemnly, he made his way to the desk.

"May I present the lady of the story, Agent Vera," and he lifted both arms and pointed to her.

Spontaneous HooRahs exploded.

"HooRah! HooRah! HooRah! HooRah! HooRah…"

Fifteen HooRahs were enough for the sergeant so he raised his hands in the air, dropped his right hand and cut it across his throat. Placing a finger in each ear, he stood before the crowd.

Agent Vera, red as Jel's red blouse below her, was shaking her head at the sergeant.

"I won't ask Agent Vera to say a few words at this time but I suspect you will hear from her sometime in the future.

"I've finished three stories. I think I have time for one more. It is the longest and hardest for me to tell. Are you ready for the last story?"

"HooRah!"

8 | *The Fourth Story*

"This is a Christmas story. Both main characters are from Puyallup. Graves, you will soon recognize who they are. All of you will know one of them before I finish."

We all loved the idea that we now knew one and would soon know another of the characters. This stuff wasn't out of one of our textbooks but was real and what life was all about.

"I have never told this story before and I am unable to say how you may like it. I hope that I am strong enough to finish it. I guarantee that you will carry it home. Here goes."

Wet sweat from Sheila's hand moistened mine and I wiped it on my pants. I could feel her anxiety matching mine. I was not sure I wanted to hear this story. For comfort, I took her hand again.

"The starting background is Puyallup High school. Two boys were continuously together: second string on the baseball team, alternating weekends at each other's houses, and sitting together in class. One had a scholarship to Seattle University and the other to the University of Washington. But they made arrangements to postpone college, went to the recruiting office and joined the U.S Army together. Both excelled in boot camp and were billeted for medical training upon boot completion of boot."

The sergeant let his eyes roam to Graves. Graves was nodding and wiping his eyes, first with his left sleeve and then his right. Tears still fell and splotched his pant legs. Many could see his display and responded to the "power-of-suggestion", and joined to make their own puddle of tears.

"After medical school, they were sent to Afghanistan. There they soon were nicknamed "Doc" because of their abilities. They alternated their assignments, literally saving a life a week. On a given day, one would travel on a scout patrol in a Humvee and the other would serve in the make-shift camp hospital attending the bed-confined. The next day, they would swap.

"Afghanistan is made up of rough terrain; Noshak Mountain is as high as 24,580 feet; compare that to our Mt. Rainier at 14,411 feet. In this terrain, the enemy can move almost at will without detection. Sure, we have satellite coverage, drones, helicopters, airplanes and all kinds of armored vehicles. Except for the satellites, all are noise makers and the enemy would be out of sight in caves or under heavy foliage at the first whisper. A full time on-sight soundless lookout was needed."

Familiar with Mt. Rainier, I tried to imagine a mountain almost two miles higher. I perked to listen as he went on.

"Kabul, Afghanistan's capital, is relatively safe but in the rest of the country are warlords, drug barons, Al-Qadir and the Taliban. As soon as the patrol leaves camp, it is at risk.

"Satellite mapping identified two caves at a high elevation on one of the mountains in the middle of a hot war zone. A photo run by a helicopter confirmed the size of the caves' mouths. Two paratroopers with oxygen were quietly inserted and later after their look-see, were lifted by copter to report one cave was satisfactory. A clearing on a cliff, 200 meters from the cave, was flat enough for a patrol drop by rope from a copter. Cliffs prevented any other means of access.

"A call for volunteers was issued and a patrol team volunteered. The patrol was outfitted. Cave reconstruction required construction equipment so the first drop was heavy and over the weight limit. Copter take off was 2300, that's 11 P.M., to allow arrival at the site in the dark. It was my patrol crew and I was the medic on the team!"

The sergeant blinked his eyes several times, bent over the desk, and wiped his face with a light brown handkerchief. As he raised his head, students could see his torment.

"At 2230, as we were loading, the radio squawked.

"Newton to the hospital pronto," were my orders.

"I'll be right back. Don't leave without me. You need a medic," I shouted as I hustled away.

"One of the wounded was taking his last breath as I arrived. He had done it before and I knew the trouble. I seized his chin, opened his mouth, 'thunked' his chest hard and, as he coughed, I yanked a candy kiss from the back of his throat. He always tried to eat three at a time and the last one would get caught. Without waiting for praise from the nurse or the soldier's thanks, I rotated and raced back to the copter. It was gone!"

"The ground crew gave me the news. 'John Ward took your place.'"

Again the sergeant bowed over the desk and wiped his face. Surmising that this was difficult for him to tell and that it was getting harder, I was afraid of what was coming.

"Yes, John Ward and I are the main characters in this story, the two Johns from Puyallup High. This is hard for me to share. Please be patient."

He paused again.

"From the TV news, you know that Afghanistan has extreme weather at times. The patrol safely made it to the cave and bad weather set in. It was mid-winter, when the temperature often is below zero, but this time it was -25 degrees in that cave.

"The patrol was equipped with a week of K-rations, oxygen and water since a second drop was scheduled three days later. Severe wind and poor visibility prevented an on-schedule second drop."

I had missed breakfast and my stomach was growling. Sheila lowered her hand to my stomach and said, "Shh." My mind was helping my stomach along as I thought of those guys in the cold without food. From scout training, I knew that there would be no wildlife for nourishment at that altitude.

"A Boeing CH47 Chinook, a heavy lift helicopter, was loaded for a try on the sixth day. The Taliban had heard the first copter and were waiting. They shot down the Chinook. The pilots were rescued.

"I'm not going to drag this out. Two weeks later, survival teams reached the cave to find an expired crew."

Sheila fell to my lap sobbing. Boys as well as girls were weeping without shame. Graves had fallen to sit on the floor, head between his knees, wailing.

"Can I tell you the rest of the story?" cried the sergeant.

Not one student responded.

"This happened the week before Thanksgiving last year. The next of kin were notified by the end of the first week in December. Early Christmas Eve, the Ward family received an anonymous telephone call."

John was the only one that survived that mountain. He will be arriving at SeaTac out of Atlanta on Delta 1061 at 9:21 P.M. Christmas day.

Tears changed from those of sorrow to those of glee. The students were clapping each other on the back. A Hoorah erupted. But the celebration quieted as the sergeant spoke his next words. There was more and we wanted to hear it.

"I happened to be on Christmas leave and the Wards invited me. They decided not to open presents. They wanted to wait for John.

"Decision time. What would you do for John?"

The sergeant took a step to approach a student at his back.

"No. That is unfair with the way we all feel. I'll make some suggestions and you nod if you agree. Okay, girls, this is for you.

"You would bake him the biggest cake that would go into the oven. Right?"

"HooRah," they responded.

"Then you would decide that he needed more so you would bake him another cake. And you would put birthday candles on each cake, 22 candles on the cake for this year, and 21 candles on the cake for the birthday he missed last year."

"HooRah!" the girls screamed.

The sergeant was weeping openly now. He didn't take the time to wipe his eyes but let the tears roll and drop to the desk and to the floor.

"And guys, you would go down to Best Buy, closed for Christmas day, break in and take the newest, fastest, biggest-screen laptop in the store. If the police came, you would invite them to the celebration. Right?"

"HooRah!" the boys boomed.

"This will be a little harder but see if you agree. Daddy would knock the side of the house out and have a red Mercedes convertible parked next to the Christmas tree. Momma would get a yellow ribbon, 12 inches wide, 60 feet long, make a bow as big as you are tall and wrap that convertible. Right?"

The room went wild. "HooRah! HooRah! HooRah…"

The soldier, his face like a wrinkled used napkin, stood at attention, glanced at Graves and then Principal Finn, and said,

"I can see that you are in a party mode. Picture with me that Christmas scene.

"The pine tree scent would permeate the room, the tree itself stretching to the high gabled ceiling, tree lights blinking their

colors on surrounding ornaments and the room's walls, and more
than 30 crowded and standing in the room. Little tykes in their red
and green Christmas duds are screaming and running about,
blowing miniature bugles. You're blinded by Mom and Sis
recording the event with camera flashes. The dining table,
expanded to 10 feet with extensions and covered with a white bed
sheet for a tablecloth, holds two immense cakes with their 21 and
22 candles waiting for a match. Plates, silverware and napkins are
stacked 10 deep several places on the table. Work-around buckets,
actually make-do kitchen pots, of ice holding bottles of champagne
are placed on boxes. The new laptop is open showing a
background display of John in his military dress fatigues and is on
a card table covered with a red tablecloth. Dad is standing next to
the Mercedes with keys in hand for John."

The sergeant paused and scanned to see if the group was
feeling the emotion that had overcome him when he heard that
John was coming home. No one was uttering a word and all eyes
were glazed with thoughts of the celebration.

"Would you like to be there?"

"HooRah! HooRah! HooRah!" we all agreed.

"It gets worse."

Worse? With that the students calmed.

"Mr. Ward rented a huge touring bus so we could all go
together. It seemed the bus would lose its top with the 28 of us
yelling, singing, tooting, and crying. The Airport police arranged
for the bus to park right at the Delta luggage claim and ushered us

by baggage screening check points to the gate. Delta personnel, as well as those from other airlines, were partying with us as the aircraft nosed to the gate. A KIRO TV camera, on airport duty for human interest stories, recorded every tear, shout, and smile.

"Each Delta 1061 passenger was greeted with cheers as he exited the tunnel. The passengers grinned and waved as the crowd treated them as returning heroes. Finally, the last passenger came through the door and the stewardess following him said,

"That's all folks."

"The airport became as quiet as a closed coffin. All were trying to see through the door. There had to be one more. Where was he? Mr. Ward ran after the stewardess and asked for the flight manifest. John's name was not on the list. I had a Delta official contact Atlanta and there had been no ticket purchased for John. We had been duped.

"Someone wanted to be mean!"

"No, oh no. Please no," a girl cried out.

"As we prepared to leave the gate in shock, the loudspeaker blared, 'John Ward, please report to the Delta counter. John Ward, please report to the Delta counter immediately.'"

"En masse, it was a marathon. I reached the Delta counter first, did not see John and asked the clerk about the page."

"We haven't paged anyone all night!" she said.

"We had been duped again!"

The sergeant sat on the desk and openly wept.

The buzzer burped again for the next class. Observing the

clock, the sergeant managed to say,

"Sorry, I don't have time to tell you who did this or why. It would take another 15 minutes. I'm short on time and have to run. I enjoyed being with you. I hope to see some of you as you come to join the fight for your country. HooRah!" and he began working his way through the crowd to the door.

Principal Finn raised an arm and stopped him.

"That was the most motivational talk I've ever heard by a guest speaker. I'm going to arrange with the U.S. Army recruiting office to delay your return so you can tour all the schools."

The sergeant gave it some thought and then said,

"Decision time, Corporals. Do I stay or fight? 'Yes', for stay. 'HooRah', for fight."

"HooRah!"

The sergeant then answered the principal, "Sorry, those are my orders. Here's your mike." He saluted the students, turned to Graves, saluted again and left.

Hearing the sergeant's reply, my heart hiccupped twice and then felt as if it had flipped completely over. My hope was walking out the door. Why couldn't he have said, "Yes, I'll hang around and do that?"

I wanted him to help with the Diangellos. With his help, a court and jail wouldn't be needed. He would take them out of the picture.

Part II

The New Year

Others often inject unexpected

curves into our paths.

9 | *Trouble*

The New Year was here and I wasn't ready. Grumpily, I fell into my seat and thought, "They better be good to me today or I'm leaving." My attitude was reflected in the solemn faces of others as they privately sought their desks. Nobody wanted to start the first class of the New Year. I wished that the soldier was back to excite us with his true-to-life stories.

I thought back to how last year had started: a severe cold windy storm, a missed bus and a wet walk to school. Fortunately, the storm did not repeat and I had caught the bus.

Hunched, pruned faced at his desk, Mr. Graves didn't enjoy the New Year any more than the rest of us. He waited 10 minutes into the class period, until all were seated and settled before he raised his head. Rivulets of tears streamed into a pond collecting on his desk. A hush fell; even the constant squawkers lost their voices.

"As I left the house this morning, I received a call from Mr. Newton, U.S. Army Staff Sergeant John Newton's father. It is with regret that I must load this on you, this first day.

"Four days after Christmas, John went on his first patrol after return to Afghanistan. The patrol was in the Panjshir Valley north of Kabul, the capital of Afghanistan. Seeing a wrecked car in the ditch, he and his crew plunged from their Humvee to aid passengers. The first passenger to be removed, a survivor who was literally wrenched from the vehicle through the broken windshield, was wandering around in a daze. He stepped on a land mine. John, knowledgeable of land mines, saw destruction coming if the passenger lifted his foot from the nipple. The blast would take out his entire crew and the passengers. The passenger stumbled off before John could reach him. John threw himself at the mine and covered it as it exploded. John's forfeit saved the lives of his crew and passengers, although all were injured.

"Look at her! Grab her! She's going to fall!" one of the students screeched, pointing at Corporal Carol.

Carol was swaying in her seat like a pendulum and as we spun to see her, she collapsed to her side on the floor.

"Sebastian, take off your sweatshirt and use it for a pillow," Mr. Graves barked as he ran for the speaker phone on the wall to call the office.

"Girl fainted in 173. Need assistance," he shouted.

A nurse and two students, carrying a stretcher, burst in within seconds. Corporal Carol was beginning to stir as they arrived. After the nurse waved smelling-salts in front of Carol's nose, she sat up and was assisted to the stretcher. As Carol was carried out, the nurse parted with the words, "She will be alright in an hour. I'll take her to the nurse's station for the time being."

With the news of the soldier's death and witnessing Carol's faint, we were all brooding. Mr. Graves could see and feel our agony. He squared his shoulders and announced,

"If you didn't hear the nurse, Carol will be alright in an hour. As for plans for John, there will not be a funeral. The Puyallup Herald will announce details of the death. You will find the time and place of a memorial service in the article. You are all invited and are excused from school to go."

"Would you stand for a moment of silence in honor of John and his sacrifice?"

Some were able to stand but most remained with their heads on their desks, sobbing in their grief.

"You may be seated. Class is cancelled. I am unable to teach."

A hand was waving, a boy.

"Yes."

"How old do you have to be to enlist?"

"I'm sorry, I don't really know. Some have been able to enlist younger with parent's permission. Enlisting without finishing high school is not good. The U.S. Army wants educated and capable soldiers. You'll do much better to wait for a diploma."

"But I don't want to see the loss of John go to waste. I want to take his place."

The door banged open. Ms. Webster, out of breath after a run from the office, barked, "Mr. Graves, please excuse Sebastian."

"Sebastian, you're excused."

Haste was expected if I read Ms. Webster's wishes correctly. Leaving books and pack, I was at her side before she could spin to the door.

She was in a race mode and headed for the office. At the office door, she slowed and urgently whispered, "We had a hold-up."

In the office, a group were circled and intently watching a computer monitor. Principal Finn pushed several aside, grasped my arm, and forced me to face the monitor.

"A masked man with a gun came to the office. Homeland Security installed a video system so we have it on DVD. You met the Diangellos and can identify them. I want to know if the assailant on the DVD is a Diangello," the principal clarified.

Someone brushed my shoulder and I glanced back. It was Ms. Webster. I reached for her hand. She had seen the Diangellos when they came to Stahl. The video was restarted and together we scrutinized every pixel as it flew by.

The video showed the assailant enter the office and hand a paper to the clerk, the shock of the clerk, and the motion of the gun as he aimed about the office. The assailant waved a hand up and down ordering everyone to lie on the floor. Clearly, he would not speak, just gave orders by motioning with his right hand.

As the video finished, Principal Finn put a hand on my back and asked,

"Sebastian, yes or no?"

"The video is fuzzy and not clear. The guy knew where the camera was and didn't expose more than his back. Sheila saw the Diangellos at Stahl so she ought to see this, too." But I knew! While Hangman was at my house, he had always held his elbow against his side, bent at 90 degrees, when waving the gun. This guy had too.

"Ms. Webster, and you, Sebastian, wait here. We'll show it again. I'll have the clerk collect Sheila," directed the principal.

It seemed to me that Principal Finn wanted to be sure that no one recognized the assailant before the police arrived. Why was that? The plot thickened. He could have said "Are you sure?" or moaned a bit but no, he was cool. My intuition was telling me "Be careful with this guy."

Smiling at me, Sheila came in. The principal told of the hold up but inadvertently added information that he hadn't told me. And a second viewing revealed more detail. The safe had been opened. Immediately, without hesitation, the thief had removed a collection bag, full of rattling change, and thrown it to the floor with a clunk. The thief sorted through miscellaneous lost-and-found junk until he found the Espinoza Family History package, snatched it and escaped through the Commons.

The three of us watched the video and as it finished, I shook my head at Sheila. Sheila noticed the odd arm posture but said "no" after I gave her a slight hug. I mouthed "Later".

Two Pierce County Sheriff Deputies and a detective strode in. Entwining my fingers with Sheila's, I led her out.

"Things are happening too fast. Did you hear about the sergeant?" I remarked as soon as we were free of the office.

"It's all over the school."

"Sheila, the library is open. Are you free this period to join me?"

"You owe me an explanation. I'm with you."

Settled in a back corner, behind shelves, I filled Sheila in on everything that I could remember about the Diangellos and the Espinozas. Then I said,

"I don't have faith in Principal Finn. His actions and what he says lead you to believe one way, but it seems to me that there is a lot that he isn't saying. For example, examine this hold-up.

1. The assailant knew of a camera! Only one person in the school officially knew it was there. Our friend.

2. The assailant knew where the camera was!

3. The assailant knew what he was after and where it was. Only the principal and three assistants, who had safe access, knew what was in the safe. How did the assailant find out?

4. The assailant avoided voice detection by not speaking. The short Diangello, I call him Hangman, speaks with a lisp. If the thief was the Hangman and he said anything, he could be identified.

"You and I both know that the assailant was the Hangman by the way he held his left arm. Ms. Webster did too because I heard her gasp when she saw the arm but she wouldn't tell the principal. To be honest with ourselves, we don't know what part the principal may play. I've already told you about the Espinoza Family History hard disk but I didn't say that I believe it is a fake. The real one is probably in a bank vault someplace."

"I agree.   But are you expecting something of me?"

"Yes.   You are my inside spy!   Keep your eyes and ears open while in the office.   It's possible that one of the assistants may be our suspect instead of the principal.   In their alertness, they may have noticed the change in the office and saw the camera. They would know what was in the safe.   An Espinoza package has no business in the safe and would stick out like a sore thumb.

"I can do that."

"Excuse me a minute." And I dialed Agent Vera.

Agent Vera answered on the first ring.   She had not heard of the theft yet.   The normal information flow delay had prevented the news from reaching her but she would request the video.   When I mentioned that I thought the school copy of the disk had been a fake, she advised me to keep it quiet.   Homeland Security had secretly opened the school safe and examined the disk and knew of its lack of authenticity.

"The video is enough to put the short Diangello behind bars if Ms. Webster, Sheila and you are willing to testify.   However, the dribbles of evidence against the tall one is not enough and we need more to nail them both.   We will wait to do it at the same time."

"I need to chat with your family.   This robbery changes things.   I'll be by your home at 8 P.M."

The buzzer announced the end of the period.   After I moved the cell from my ear, Sheila kissed my cheek, and then reassured me, "We'll get them!"   She bent, snatched her pack and was gone.

Cheek?   Was I losing ground?

In the break between 3rd and 4th periods, I snared Juan.

"Did you hear about the hold-up this morning? Someone stole the Espinoza disk from the school safe."

"Jel told me. She had a note from Principal Finn to come to the office and heard there."

"Keep your eyes peeled. The trouble is just starting."

As I walked to my next class, Jel arm-twisted me to a wall and demanded, "You know what this means? They'll raid my house next. You knew that the disk was a counterfeit, didn't you? What can I do now?"

She was at her wits end and thought that I could save her since she thought that I had done it before. I wanted to say that it would all be alright, that there was nothing to fear. But I decided the words would be meaningless.

After her outbreak, she had calmed but wasn't releasing my arm. It was as if super glue had crystallized and the seal could only be fractured with a sledge hammer and chisel.

"I agree that a Diangello brand tribulation will be initiated the moment they read the disk. Yes, I strongly suspected the disk was a gambit and anticipated this coming. I am meeting with Agent Vera tonight. But in the meantime, do you have a gun in the house?"

"We have two, a Glock 45 pistol and a 22 semi-automatic rifle. I have practiced with both," she replied.

"I'd keep both loaded with a bullet in the chamber, with full magazines and with their safety off. I would position them out of reach of children but next to the doors in the kitchen and living room. For clear unobstructed earshot to other members of the family, I'd keep internal doors open."

"Here's my and Agent Vera's cell numbers. After meeting with Agent Vera tonight, I'll call you."

I handed her my 3x4 spiral pad so she could jot down her phone number.

"Are you still keeping a record of when and where you see the Diangellos? I need it tonight."

She fussed in her purse and handed me a piece of paper, folded in quarters

"I'll get Juan's for you by lunch."

I leaned away to pick up my pack and the super glue broke. But, she wasn't done. She clinched me, kissed me hard, and whispered in my ear, "Thank you, my hero." The bolt from the sky had struck again. Then, giving me a look that said more than I could understand, she let go and ran off.

My paranoia worried me all day. At my locker, as I was leaving, I found Juan's 3x4 spiral pad, the cover torn by its insertion through the quarter-inch door slots.

At home, Mom, excited with company coming, wanted to delay dinner for when Agent Vera could be here. Sarah had missed lunch and wanted to eat on time so we all swallowed our meals whole so we would be finished with the clean-up when Agent Vera arrived. As 8 P.M. approached, Sarah was excused and we stretched out in the living room, pretending that we weren't nervous. My right foot had a rhythm all its own. Finally, I said,

"The school safe was robbed today. Agent Vera's visit is related to the robbery."

Dad, more anxious than any of us, queried,

"Did they get anything? Did the thief get away?"

"Yes to both of your questions. We'll…"

The Star Spangled Banner overrode our discussion. I invited Agent Vera in and pointed to the throne, the fanciest plush chair.

"I have another meeting so we'll not waste time with hellos, nice-to-see-you and how-have-you-been.

"The Emerald Ridge High School office was robbed at gun point today by a single assailant. He didn't speak but Sebastian identified him in a video to be the short Diangello that visited your home."

Turning to face Dad and then Mom, she said,

"The intruder held his arm like this." She demonstrated by lifting her gun from a shoulder holster with her left hand and placing her left elbow at her side with the arm cocked at 90 degrees.

"Would you be willing to identify him on a video if asked in a court of law?"

Both nodded. She went on.

"The thief demanded the safe be opened, discarded a cloth money bag and filched the Espinoza Family History hard disk. The disk was reported to have evidence that could be used by Los

Angeles Police to arrest a suspect in a bombing. The assailant fled from the office out through the Commons and disappeared.

"You will have questions about Emerald Ridge High's safe security. Unfortunately, Homeland Security hired a private firm to install the security camera after a recent break-in attempt. The private firm wanted to sell the product and advertised its installation which showed pictures of the camera and its coverage. Thus, school security was breached. With several school administrators having access to the safe, the disk retention in the safe was not a secret. It was like, 'Here it is; come get it.'

"When the Diangellos find that they have been conned, that the disk is counterfeit, we expect them to take stronger steps. That's why I am here tonight."

Mom, with an open mind, asked, "Who are the Diangellos?"

"I'm sorry. I'm limited on what I can tell you."

At which Mom said, "Who are their family? Are they married and do they have children? Where do they live? Do they work and where? Surely that information is public domain and you can tell us."

"Yes, I can share that. Diangellos originated in Napoli, Italy. The original family lives there and operates a community very similar to that in Los Angeles, only on a much larger scale. They are not a part of the strong Italian Mafia but are recognized as a sister representing Napoli. Because of terrorist concerns, the CIA has visibility of their operation.

"When World War II peace treaties were being written, three Diangello brothers emigrated from Italy to Chicago and then to Los Angeles. They married Americans and have families. Estimates put the Los Angeles group size at 50 to 60.

"Two sons, born in Los Angeles of one of the brothers, moved to our area. They are not married. They live within a mile of your home, in Devoreaux. They work as afternoon doormen in a Seattle apartment complex from 3 to 10 P.M., seven days a week. They split days and rotate days back and forth. They drive to work and the one not on duty drives around and makes various stops all over the Seattle area. The guard duty requires that they be armed so they carry and have a license to do so."

"They scare me to death. The way they look, I'd be afraid to live in the apartment if I had to face them," I said.

"Four complaints have been filed by residents. Each was because the brother on duty placed his hand on his holster as a resident tried to pass without proper credentials."

Agent Vera reviewed what she had said and then asked,

"Any more questions? No?"

"Yes, how do the Diangellos know about the disk and what's on it?" Dad wanted to know.

"You have asked a question that pertains to our investigation but I can't answer because I don't know. It is standard practice for a business to have a back up system and I suspect that is what the Diangellos are looking for. As a side note, Fernandez removed the store computer's hard disk at the end of each shift anticipating a possible computer theft during the night. That disk was destroyed in the Los Angeles house bombing.

"The Los Angeles Police reported that the store has remained intact except the computer was taken. The computer, missing the hard disk, disappeared about a week after the house bombing, long after the Espinozas departed. You can guess who probably took it.

"As the Diangellos become more desperate, they are becoming more violent. We are guessing that they would blow up the Espinozas' house if they were certain that the disk is there. To this point, they haven't taken that step."

Trying to out-guess what the Diangellos might do, I let a thought ooze from my mouth, "Shotgun?"

Agent Vera heard me. "Yes, we are concerned that they have initiated a "shotgun" approach; blast anything on the path until they find it. The first shot was the school safe. They will discover that the robbery was a failure. Espinoza's home or family will be next. That brings up the second reason I wanted to come tonight."

She was changing the subject while leaving us hanging. Were the Espinozas protected? Why didn't Fernandez hand in the disk? It dawned on me that the second disk, a mere store ledger, would not provide evidence to support the arrest of Caterpillar Eyebrows. We needed evidence specifically on Caterpillar Eyebrows as we now had on the Hangman.

"The FBI has been providing 24/7 surveillance of the

Diangello brothers. Since their activity has slowed down, the 24/7 surveillance was reduced to 24/7 'on-demand' surveillance. The trigger for surveillance comes from me. And in turn, you, Sebastian, have been my source. The school robbery may restore a higher surveillance level but I don't hold any hope. More surveillance will only be imposed if there is a demand. The demand level that is necessary is dictated by the on-site reports that we get from you. At this time, there is not enough activity to warrant an increase in the surveillance level."

I handed her the two spiral pads and Jel's paper.

"Here are their activities to date."

That pushed her button.

"From now on, I want a record of every time you see them. These logs are perfect; they include times and locations. Was this your idea, Sebastian?"

I nodded.

She glanced at my folks to see if it had sunk in and said,

"I'm done and can be on my way. Do you need some more pads? Yes? How many?"

"Five. Jel, Juan, Sheila, Ms. Webster and I need one.

"Ms. Webster?"

"She's keeping secrets from Principal Finn so I thought she might be willing to watch for the Diangellos."

"Let's pass on Ms. Webster. She is a suspect."

Dad spoke as Agent Vera was leaving. "With the 'on-demand' 24/7 surveillance, there is a delay before an officer can be here. Are we authorized to shoot if the Diangellos come while we wait?"

"Do you have guns in the house?" Agent Vera inquired, showing concern in her eyes.

"Yes, two, and they will be loaded with a bullet in the chamber and with the safety off. One will be there on the top of that six-foot book case and the other on top of that tall china cabinet."

"I don't have the authority to say you can shoot, but if it were me, I wouldn't hesitate." With that, the agent hurried to her SUV: I followed her. She shuffled in the back seat, handed me six spiral pads with "Homeland Security" engraved in gold on their covers, and left.

As I entered the house, I caught Dad placing the guns. Without stopping or commenting, I passed and headed for bed.

Before retiring, I contacted Jel as I promised and said that we'd talk tomorrow. I then concentrated on the events of the day. Trouble had arrived with the opening of the first class, had continued during the day, and now there was no end in sight. I wondered what the sergeant would do if he were in my shoes. I couldn't guess but I wished that I could carry one of those guns in my backpack.

10 | *Offense*

After the terrible day on Monday, I fought the morning. Skipping a day from school was not an option so I gave in and prepared for breakfast. Sarah was her normal boisterous self but sensed the depressing mood. As she finished her toast and prepared to leave the table, Dad said,

"Sarah. Would you do something for me? Please take someone with you when you are outside. Something has come up that threatens our family and we need to be super careful. Will you do this for me?"

"What's up?"

"We'll inform you tonight. Okay?"

Worry wasn't in her persona. Nodding, she bounced from the table and went her way. Dad winked at me and I followed, grabbed my pack, and moved out for the bus.

Swamped by black hovering clouds all about me, I was gasping for air. I considered the benefits of a meeting. Would it lighten my mood? I had the Homeland Security pads and I could pass them out all at once. At school, I scheduled a lunch meeting with Sheila, Amin, Jel, and Juan in the cafeteria. With the agenda firm in my head, I went to greet them.

Sheila arrived late but showing a "got-you" grin.

"Before we start I have news! The shorter Diangello was

the thief. He scraped skin and hair from his arm on the safe's hinge and DNA identified it."

Hangman being the thief was old news to Sheila and me, but Jel and Juan were delighted.

Jel had dreamed of news like this and said, "Now, they can put him in jail."

"No, I don't think they will. The target is both Diangellos and they will want to wait to trap them together," I discouraged her.

While I had the floor, I opened the meeting.

"The purpose of this meeting is to update you with the latest."

As I passed out the Homeland Security pads, I said,

"Agent Vera needs a record of the times and locations of all Diangello sightings. The information will define a pattern and be used to alert the FBI if a change in surveillance is needed.

"The FBI were the ones providing 24/7 surveillance but with the reduced activity in the last month, the 24/7 surveillance was reduced to 24/7 'on-demand' surveillance. Agent Vera generates almost all of the demands. In turn, we are Agent Vera's eyes and thus we spawn most of the surveillance requests. Jel and Juan, I passed our sighting logs to Agent Vera last night. She was overjoyed to say the least and asked that we all do it."

"My cell number is 253 227-5963 and is noted on the first page of your pad. I keep the cell on me 24/7. I have all of your home phone numbers but you should exchange them among yourselves. Call someone if there is trouble."

Amin had been silent but wanted to make a contribution.

"From you, I hear that we should call if anything happens, record sightings, and don't get caught. With our overlooking, watchful task, let's call our group the "Hawks" and meet like this every Tuesday."

He went on, "We need code names if we use the phone. It must be something simple. For names, let's assign numbers as we are seated around the table. SEBie is 1, Sheila 2, me 3, Jel 4 and Juan 5.

We all agreed. I jotted in my pad:

SEBie 1

Sheila 2

Amin   3

Jel   4

Juan   5

"And we need a communication system. I propose a chain in case one person is being monitored. 1 will pass information to 4, 4 to 5, and so on. If contact is not made to the next party, then contact the following number. Don't use the chain except for crisis matters, like the robbery."

Amin's training when with his father in the Washington DC embassy was strengthening our group. We were becoming a spy network. I hadn't thought that far ahead.

"Any more 3?" I asked.

"No. Wait--yes. Protect all this with your life! Discard the pads if it appears that you will be caught with it. It may result in harm to the whole group if it is leaked. Okay, I'm done," Amin ended.

"To enlighten you, Amin has specialized training in this field. He will likely prove to be an invaluable asset for us.

"We are now on offense. If the FBI won't step up to the plate and swing, we will. Meeting over," I said to close the meeting. We picked up our back packs and parted individually.

Later to test the chain, I nabbed Sheila and said, "This is a chain test. Agent Vera says that she can't authorize a shooting but she wouldn't hesitate!"

By the end of the day, Juan shouldered close and muttered, "This is a chain test. Agent Vera says she would shoot." The chain was working and fast.

Entering the house, two pairs of eyes bore through me, Sarah's and Mom's.

"Is it true that you found a $3,000,000 purse? And muggers are trying to take it away from you?" Sarah cried.

"Yes, but I returned it to the owner."

"You didn't keep any of the money?"

"No."

"My hero!" Sarah said and she threw her arms about me.

"Sarah, have you seen a tan Hyundai at the bus stop or driving around Stahl?"

"No. Is that the mugger's car?"

"Yes. Please tell me if you see it." I was sure that Mom

had advised her of their threat.

Breaking free, I hauled my pack of books to my room. When I finished my homework, my thoughts tumbled. The Diangello dilemma was blurring my mind. I resolved to develop a plan to trap the tall Diangello, Caterpillar Eyebrows, now that we had snared the shorter, Hangman. I moved from my desk to my thinking throne, my bed.

As I brainstormed, TV mystery programs were appearing. Yes, it made me sleepy and dozing became a deep sleep. I dreamed of a body laying in a field and someone planting evidence.

"Sebastian! Dinner," Dad shouted through the door. I awoke and knew that I had dreamed but couldn't remember the dream.

Stewing through dinner, I was in a stupor trying to recall that dream. It wouldn't reveal itself. I gave up and joined the conversation about me. Sarah was quizzing Dad but he left it to Mom to provide the answers. Aware that she was being shunted by Dad, Sarah turned to me and said,

"Sebastian, can you help me out here?"

"Sarah, in the big picture, this involves more than me finding a $3,000,000 purse. It entails an Italian Mafia connection, a Los Angeles gang, national security and possibly terrorism. It is very serious. For example, one of the muggers robbed Emerald High School on Monday. Nobody has answers to the questions that you are asking. If they did, there would be mass arrests, a lot more than just our two muggers. The more you know, the tighter the noose will be if you are kidnapped and the higher the risk to the family. Mom has probably told you more than she should have. Do yourself and me a favor. Keep this a family secret. I'll answer one more question before we cut this off."

Sarah was looking at me in shock with her mouth half open. I believed that I had to put a scare into her so that she would be willing to maintain an envelope of secrecy. I felt that our family's lives depended on it.

"No more questions? Good. But I'll answer one that you will have after this sinks in. Yes, we are working with authorities: Homeland Security, FBI, CIA and the Pierce County Sheriff. Homeland Security and Pierce County Sheriff deputies have been here in our home several times."

Knowing the secrets that Sarah had kept last year when I had been at Stahl, I was confident that this 12 year old would keep her lips sealed.

"Sarah, I didn't tell you this to scare you but to be sure that you look out for your own safety. Okay, the discussion is ended." I left the table for my room. Subsequent to that, all that could be heard from the kitchen was the clatter of dishes.

After I retired, I sought ideas on how to deal with the Diangellos. Brain dead, I drifted to sleep without an answer.

At breakfast, Sarah's eyes were full of sleep. She came to me and placed her arm at my waist, giving me a squeeze. Words weren't needed.

The dream came back to me as the bus traveled by the open fields. A body in a field was what it was. While spinning the dream in my head, ideas formed like reflections in a dark store window when a police car's revolving lights pierce warnings to a break-in intruder. The root to a plan had appeared in a dream.

On each of the following days, I dedicated an hour each day to researching and plotting. I borrowed mysteries from the library to expand my knowledge. Piece by piece, the plot formed. As a beginner in the world of crime, I felt anything could go wrong. Unseen and unknown events could not be predicted and I was afraid that my plan might result in one of the Hawks or a member of a family being hurt or killed.

The Hawks continued to meet weekly and the meetings were short. They disbanded within a few minutes. Except for the recordings of Diangello sightings, nothing had transpired.

One night, I concluded that there was no point in taking more steps if things remained quiet. Although our offensive team was prepared, we would remain stagnant and wait.

11 | *Break-in*

"The Diangellos are at my house. They are taking Juan."

I recognized Jel's voice and said, "I'll have the police there pronto."

I kept the line open on my cell and ran to the house phone and dialed Agent Vera.

"Agent Vera."

"The Diangellos are kidnapping Juan from the Espinozas. I have Jel on my cell."

"The police will be there in five minutes. I'll be there in 60."

When she spoke, I had the cell glued to the house phone.

"Jel, did you hear that?"

"Yes. Someone's coming," and Jel was gone.

"Thanks, Agent. Bye." I replaced the house phone and called Sheila.

"Hello, Sheila speaking."

"2, Diangellos are at Espinozas and are kidnapping Juan. More information will follow." With that, I had told her all that I knew. Brevity was key. I checked the front yard in case they came to my house next. I clutched the gun from the bookcase and then peeped through the front window drapes.

After an hour, I replaced the gun and retraced my steps to

my desk. Determined to implement my plan the next day, I typed out a "Capture Caterpillar Eyebrows" strategy on the computer. In this last feat, the Diangellos had gone one step too far. The plan would work even if Juan was still a captive. I would have to find a replacement for Juan and I was hoping Lynn would agree. If she would, we could kick-off the plan.

At midnight, the news from the Espinozas came on my cell. Jel was elated. Juan had escaped. Her story was:

Our family had been to the Puyallup Public Library and when we entered the house, the Diangellos stepped from the bathroom and the kitchen with their guns pointing at Dad.

"Hand over the disk," the tall one ordered.

Dad told him, "Can't do it. It's not here."

"Then, we'll go after it."

Not intimidated by the show of power, Dad waited for a minute. Antsy, the short one was dance stepping, left-right-left...and I thought that he was going to butt in.

"The disk is in a place that is not available at this time. I couldn't get it now if I lived in the White House," Dad threw in their faces.

"The Diangellos moved to stand next to the couch and whispered back and forth. Standing close, I could hear most of what they said. At first, the shorter one argued that Dad was lying. Soon, the tall one had the upper hand and asked,

"Do the police have it?"

"No."

"How long before it is available?"

"My guess is four weeks. The party involved is in South Africa on an aid mission. There is not a formal schedule for his tour. He said when he left that he didn't know the date of his homecoming and that he would stay as long as the money holds out. Funds are coming in daily which extends his trip indefinitely.

As an expert in inventing tales, I thought that this one took the prize. Jel was like a recorder and kept going.

The short one was on edge and upset. He said,

"Wilbur, we have to have it in four weeksh. If we don't have that dishk, we'll never be able to…"

"Shut up, you fool," the tall one said.

The Diangellos had another private confab. This one took a little longer so they sat on the couch. They concluded that they could scare Dad into speeding up the acquisition.

"We're going to take the boy with us. If the disk is not available in 2 weeks, that's 14 days from now at 8 P.M.; we will chop off a toe and send it special delivery the next day. It will be a toe a day and then his fingers. After that his ears. Then his teeth. We are not waiting a year. Do you hear me?"

I didn't know how brave Juan was until that moment. I was crying but he was just gritting his teeth.

I pictured the two and almost cheered. I wished I was closer to get one of those kisses.

Then the tall one gave instructions to make sure the street was clear and take Juan to the car. The tall one stayed and secured the fort by keeping his gun on Dad. I think he knew we had a gun in the house.

As the short one prodded Juan to the car, Juan was meek as a kitten. At the car, the Diangello threw Juan across the back seat, slammed the door, and arched down to see if Juan had been hurt. Then the short one straightened and looked to the right and left to be sure that the street was still clear. Satisfied, he spun to watch for his brother.

As the short one scanned the street, Juan scooted to the opposite door. The car's interior light flashed on the instant the short one turned his back. By the time the short one repositioned himself to look through the window, all he saw was Juan's back leg as he exited the car.

At that point I was standing and cheering. I hoped that I hadn't interrupted the story but it was okay; Jel didn't slow down.

Juan knows the neighborhood well and he vanished in the side yard of the house across the street. Short One let out a yell and sprang after Juan but didn't have a chance. Juan was long gone. The tall one had also given chase but it was like a housewife trying to swat a fly. The fly knows where to hide.

The Diangellos weren't through. They marched to the front door with their pistols at their sides. Dad and Mom had seen Juan clear the car and greeted the Diangellos as the door opened. Dad had the Glock and Mom the 22, both pointed at the Diangellos' foreheads.

During target practice, Dad always told me that you can't

miss from less than five feet, hardly ever miss at six feet, and are sure of a hit if under seven feet. Those guns were four feet away.

Dad said, "The safeties are off and we're ready. Go to your car and don't come back."

They did.

Fernandez was one tough battle combatant.

Dad inspected the house. A broken dining room window appeared to be the way the Diangellos had entered.

Two Pierce County Sheriff Deputies arrived 5 minutes after I spoke to you and issued an APB for the tan Hyundai. They interrogated us until Agent Vera arrived. The three conferred and the deputies are now in their vehicle in front of our house. Agent Vera handed me her business card and left. She didn't give one to Mom and Dad and I wondered about that.

Juan waited and quietly came in the back after everybody had gone. Dad called him a scamp.

"Jel, thanks to Juan's agility and quick thinking, you dodged a bullet. I hope attempted kidnapping is enough to get Homeland Security, or whoever, off their butt to do something. Since the Diangellos sat on the couch, forensics can prove their presence; it's not just your word against theirs now.

"You might want to alert Agent Vera that you're saving the couch for the forensic team."

I was washed out and had no spark left to talk longer.

"Thanks for the call, Jel. It means a lot to me to be in the loop. We'll share this at the next Hawk meeting. I recorded your call. Good night."

Joining the family at breakfast was a pain after my late night but I was there early with my portable radio-cassette player. The recording played as we ate. The only response was from Dad.

"I hope that puts those clowns in jail."

At school, I requested another Hawk meeting.

"You need to be aware of this," I told my cohorts and I played the recording. Jel was so proud of Juan that she insisted on holding his hand. Upon its completion, Amin dampened our glee with,

"It doesn't mean a thing. They'll be booked but be out on bail before the ink dries. Excuse me! It does mean something. They'll be angrier than a swarm of bees and will be more desperate. They impersonated officers, hacked school computers, robbed the school safe and now attempted a kidnapping. Each action was a step higher in violence. Could it be that they will bomb the Espinozas' house to eliminate the disk and then go after the guy on the humanitarian quest in South Africa? By the way, for some reason, I don't believe the South African story.

"It is my opinion that the reason they want the disk is twofold. Yes, because it is evidence. But I also think that when they placed the order for bomb materials in Los Angeles, they listed the exact amounts of increments necessary for an unusual homemade bomb. From what Juan says, the bomb used to destroy the Espinozas' house wiped out everything and left a three foot hole. That is not the level of destruction generated by a garden variety homemade bomb, fabricated from information online. I suspect they are hurting because they discarded the formula after that first bomb in Los Angeles. They need the disk to re-create the formula. Is my thinking screwy?"

We all held our breath as we digested that synopsis. Amin had to be right based on what the short one had said, *"Wilbur, we have to have it in four weeks. If we don't have that disk, we'll never be able to..."*

Amin's allegations brought a fresh depth to the threats. If true, another bomb was planned and the question was "Where would it be used?" Agent Vera's reference to national security had new meaning. Were the Diangellos tied to terrorists? Was the target one of the military installations here in Washington, Joint Base Lewis-McChord or maybe the Triton submarine base on the Peninsula? Or was the objective something else like the Space Needle, or maybe one of the stadiums: Safeco or Qwest. My bet was that the first target would be the Espinozas' home.

My logic concluded that the bomb was intended for the Seattle area. I questioned that these two had the where-with-all, brains or abilities, to do anything but menial tasks. If the bomb menace was real, others had to be involved. My strategy to incriminate Caterpillar Eyebrows began to fizzle and dry up. Caterpillar Eyebrows was only one cog in a big wheel and what I had developed would certainly skew Homeland Security's maneuvers to nab the entire bomb wielding bunch.

The real world of crime and its sinister ways were trickling into my mind. The Diangellos had a get-out-of-jail-free card, a temporary clemency, while they were being used as bait by Homeland Security to catch the controllers. The temporary clemency would be made permanent if the Diangellos turned state evidence when arrested. We'd never be rid of these two.

Withholding information, claiming the standard "national security" cop out, Agent Vera could be credited with going-by-the-book. However, Amin's security training had made it possible for the Hawks to break the ice and we five were now aware of the real threat that was challenging us. Observing the consternation on each face, I was conscious that all were tuned to the same frequency and knew we were out-gunned.

"Hello, you five. What sinister schemes are you plotting?" the principal shouted. The cafeteria was noisy but not loud enough to justify him exhibiting that he had lungs any lion would be proud of. His blast from above us was as if the sky was falling and we would be squashed.

Astonished and overwhelmed, we all reared in our chairs; Juan fell backwards. We raised our eyes to see the principal leaning against our table.

"Juan saw a low flying airplane and we were thrashing out if we should hike down into the gulley to see if it crashed. The vote was a draw and my vote would break the tie. I haven't voted yet. We were thinking about what penalties would be imposed if we skipped class," I replied.

The four Hawks were shocked at my lie.

"Don't waste your time. The gulley is a Pierce County solid wasted disposal site and is full of rats. The airplane at low altitudes is an attempt to spray the rats. The rats themselves have to be doused directly for it to be effective. It's another hair brained idea from some desk jockey. The engine noise scares the rats into their holes and they are not affected." He laughed at our "yuk-rats" expression as he departed. I laughed up my sleeve because there was no airplane.

I thought back to what we might have been saying when the principal stunned us. After Amin's revelations, our minds were on hold and no one had spoken for five minutes. No, Principal Finn had not overheard anything.

"We'll meet in the Orchestra room next time and every other time after that. It is always vacant during lunch hours. Our weekly meetings are beginning to draw attention to us."

It bothered me that a simple thing like eating lunch together could raise questions. If I learned anything through all of this, it was that you had to search for the good and bad; both were there. And you could spot both if you knew where to look. The principal's chance arrival and rude greeting were a warning, a bad one in my book. Although it was not clear why, the principal made me uneasy.

"Sebastian."

"Earth to Sebastian. What's eating you?" Sheila queried.

"And I want the truth," she said laughing. "I didn't know you were the devil's brother when it came to cover-ups."

"I was milling over the arrival of the principal and what it might mean." I leaned past Sheila and took Jel's hand.

"Admit it. Your Dad's story about South Africa wasn't the truth either, was it?"

"I don't know. It was the first I'd heard it though."

Carrying a lot on our minds, we picked up our books and departed for class. Juan, headed for the classroom adjacent to mine, caught me and asked,

"The Diangellos will get off, won't they?"

I could see hope in his eyes for a negative answer.

"Right," I said, disappointing him.

"Is there anything that we can do?"

"Let's start looking farther out. Maybe we can identify their controllers. Also, logging sightings of the Diangellos will continue to help," I responded and it gave him hope.

12 | *Babysitting*

On a Thursday evening, while studying in my room, Mom hollered, "Sebastian, get out here and answer the freaking phone." With a workload of studies, my home entrance had been sleuth style to avoid 30 minutes of school update chatter. An hour later, Mom, out of character, had shouted her angry tirade.

Something had triggered her. My mind went into overdrive. It was only on extreme occasions that Mom flipped out and this was one of those times. When it happened, there was always due cause and I hoped that I wasn't the cause. Being from Mars, I didn't have the tools to deal with it. But I could try.

I reasoned that I had three choices.

- Submit like a wimp. Go and take my medicine but avoid a patronizing "you're right." A wimp tactic never worked before but there was always a first.

- Join the fit club. Throw the stinging remarks back. Dad absolutely prohibited this. "She's your mother. You do that and you deal with me."

- Wait for cooler heads to prevail. The waiting phone call prevented a delay.

So I bit the bullet and made my way to the kitchen to take my medicine.

As I walked in to pick up the phone, I saw what had incited her anger. It was justified. Mom was in the middle of preparing for the annual Friday neighborhood women's gathering; she was making a cake. She always made it the night before to be sure it was fresh and not soggy.

On our block, there were 10 houses. The community was so small that the residents knew the neighbor dog's names. All-day homemakers lived in four, working wives in the other six. Without fail, every year Mom sent invitations and all ten came. I thought that the ladies came for the cake, not the session. Visitors were not welcome. I construed that visitors weren't welcome because there wasn't enough cake. The cake was an 8x15 flat cake that was cut into 20 2x3 inch squares. The meeting opened with each having a piece of cake to set the mood. And, unvaryingly, all would have seconds before departure. One lady insisted on licking the pan and finishing the crumbs.

One year, a woman brought her sister. Mom simply cut one 2x3 piece in half and served the halves to the woman and her sister. That night after the meeting, Mom shared at the dinner table that the woman was angry.

As the lady left, she spewed, "If you weren't such a skinflint, you'd make two cakes so we could all have our fill."

Mom replied without batting an eye, "Skinflint? If you'd eat at home, you wouldn't have to eat here." The lady has come back for her cake every year.

So here Mom was, baking her favorite dark chocolate cake

for dessert. She called it her "chocolate mushroom cake". She created it from scratch: dark-dark chocolate from Trader Joes, organic eggs, and heavy cream. It was a three layer cake with a layer of dark chocolate pudding from Switzerland as the center layer.

Why mushroom? She had a tube of tablets that she spread on a grid in the pudding layer before pouring on the top chocolate layer. When baked, the pellets swelled and popped the cake up like mushrooms. Decorated with walnuts on each swell, the cake didn't need icing. Timing was critical as the layers were laid or the mushrooms didn't grow.

"You could have come and answered the phone. I'm not the secretary, you know. Tell your friend that she spoiled my cake and I have to make another."

If I said I was sorry, it would add to the problem so I quietly reached for the phone. Yes, the phone was an old one with a corded handset so Mom would hear every word and she yearned to.

"Hello."

"Sebastian? This is Mrs. Weeback from Devoreaux. Do you know who I am? We talked in the street last year."

"Yes, I remember you well."

"Oh, you're such a nice young man. That's why I called you. I need to ask for a favor."

Mom had stopped her cooking and pinned her head next to mine to hear. I switched the audio from the handset to the speaker.

"I'd be glad to help you in any way that I can."

"I have to be away for a week or two.   It's my granddaughter. She has jury duty and needs someone to care for her two children. Could you baby sit my house?"

Mom was nodding.

"Okay, will do."

"You won't have to do a thing! All the meals you need are in the refrigerator and freezer. Instructions are pasted on each box. I do ask that you clean up after yourself in the kitchen everyday to keep the odors down. I have a guest room with a TV, DVR, stereo, DVD/CD player, computer work station, and its own bath so you will be comfortable. You have free roam of the house and anything goes. Would you like to do this?"

"Be glad to. Oh, are the Diangellos still living across the street?"

"Thank you for the reminder, Sebastian. Yes, but you will not be seen by them. I have arranged with my backdoor neighbors to cross their yard and enter through the back gate. They have a paved sidewalk from the street to the gate. The walk is bounded by bushes and is private.

"It's because of the Diangellos that I need to have a sitter. This is my first time.

"All kinds of crazy doings are going on over there. There's a black SUV; I think it's a Cadillac, which disturbs my sleep. I sleep in the front room and hear everything through my window. You will too from the guest room."

I thought of what I had said to Juan. "We have to look farther." Hardy-har. This would be perfect. By literally sitting in the Diangello front yard, I might discover a controller's name.

"I'll drop by on my way from school tomorrow. It will be about 4 P.M."

"I'll watch for you. Good bye."

Without comment, Mom swallowed the idea of me being so close to the Diangellos.

"Sebastian, would you wash up the mixer and the pans while I start collecting ingredients for the next cake?"

Her anger was gone and my help restored harmony. With the good accord, I wrote my cell phone on a scrap of paper and slipped it under a magnet on the refrigerator door.

"Mom, Agent Vera wants me to carry a cell phone and here's the number," and held my finger to it.

She raised her head up once and but was in the middle of her cake mixing. I didn't care if she hadn't heard me.

* * * * *

With no difficulty, after school on Friday, I was able to catch bus number 9 to Devoreaux and Mrs. Weeback was waiting at the back door as I knocked. She embraced me as if I were her grandson.

"You are such a nice young man. I'm going to pay you, you know. Is fifty cents a day enough?"

"It's unacceptable. I refuse to accept anything."

"Are you certain? Okay let's take a tour."

The house was a mini-castle. The food was fit for a king. She had satellite TV with over 200 channels. Every room, except closets, had a TV and phone, even the bathrooms. A full set of tools were in the garage which she said she kept for repairmen.

"Make yourself to home. Don't expose yourself to roll the garbage out for pickup. The six cans are empty and with what little that you have, you'll only use one or two.

"You can have friends over. There are six bedrooms with twin and king beds. The beds are all made. My room is a girls-only room. Please don't sponsor parties. Things get broken or stolen if that occurs."

I couldn't imagine what it would be like to stay here for one night, and it was going to be for a week or more.

As she talked, she led me to front rooms on the second floor. With her walker, she was up the steps faster than if she had an elevator.

"This is my room." Plush didn't describe it. It was a female room with all the frills.

"This is your room. Don't worry about messing it up. I have a housekeeper who loves the extra hours."

I went to the window and there was the Diangellos' house, bigger than life. The jutting garage was less than 100 feet away.

Then I scanned the room. The bed was a king, so large that my whole family could sleep on it. The pillows were long and fat like the burlap bags you see in a feed store. Being used to a narrow bunk bed with a hand-me-down mattress from Dad's college days so well used that I could see the other side in several worn-thin places, I gasped. I wondered which direction on the bed I would find myself in the morning.

"Binoculars are in the desk. Come on, I want to show you the freezer."

In the kitchen, she stepped to a wall and pushed a button. A seven foot door in the wall sprang open and a gust of freezing air made me shiver. Five shelves were stacked with packages, all marked with names and cooking instructions.

"One time, my house was used for a one week seminar and we ran out of food. Since then, I have stocked enough to feed 20 for a week

"I'm all thumbs when I cook so my food is prepared to make things easy. Please eat as much as you can. I cycle the food in my freezer once a year and by the time I return, it will be time to replace it. Anything that is here when I come back will be thrown out."

Reading the labels, my imagination soared. The contents of the freezer were beyond my ability to describe. I thought of my mother's penny-pinching shopping. I realized every meal, breakfast or dinner, which I had in the next week, would be something that I might have at home once a month, if then.

"Impromtu Gourmet equips and cares for my freezer. I open the garage door once a week and they wheel in a cart with their weekly specials. I don't know what is in here. The Impromtu Gourmet house delivery is cancelled for two weeks so you won't be disturbed.

"You will be eating away from home and here in this blue bowl is money for your school lunches."

She thought of every thing.

I never dreamed that anyone could live like this. But, with this level of support, her frailty would not be a problem.

She placed her index finger on a bulletin board. "All the phone numbers you might need are listed here, including my cell and contact in Lodge Pole, Montana." After placing keys in my jacket pocket, she said,

"I will meet a taxi out the back gate tomorrow at 2 P.M. Can you be here to see me off?"

"It's Saturday. I'll be here by 1 P.M."

"My itinerary and address while in Lodge Pole are on the bulletin board. I fly to Great Falls then travel by auto to Lodge Pole. Actually, I look forward to the auto trip since they have a new Escalade.

"Do not hesitate to call. I know your hours and I will call you if I think of something."

She hugged me again and I said goodbye.

* * * * *

She was waiting again as I knocked on the door the next day. I explored the house to see if I had overlooked anything. At 1:45, I joined her in her bedroom and toted her bags to the back door. She hobbled down the stairs, her walker tap-tapping. Her two wheel walker had four inch wheels and she'd attack an obstacle like she couldn't wait to show it who is boss.

She was smiling as she waved goodbye from the taxi.

I'd been holding my breath for this moment. My anticipation, held in check for the two days since Mrs. Weeback's call, exploded and adrenaline surged with each exhalation of breath. Hastily, I ran to my room, opened the blinds, cracked the window and started my watch. I probed every drawer of the desk before I found high powered binoculars.

I sketched the landscape, marking hiding places and escape routes. Shrubs were over eight feet tall and 12 feet wide. Although they blocked my view of most of the yard, they offered unlimited hiding places. I noted the soft spots in the yard to avoid risk of leaving tracks. I drew in the location of the streetlights, one a half-block away in each direction. Not missing the fact that mailboxes were grouped to a mail-stand every block or so, I suspected that the Diangellos' mail box was in the station a half-block west.

The view from the second story window of my room exceeded my wildest dream. I tried Mrs. Weeback's window but decided mine was far better because it was 15 feet closer. However, the angle from Mrs. Weeback's window did extend sight to reach corners not visible from my room.

I returned to my room to examine the Diangellos' house.

The windows were still blacked out as I had seen last year. It appeared that black plastic garbage bags had been trimmed to fit the windows and sealed inside with two inch pieces of brown packing tape. Installation sloppiness allowed the brown tape to be seen on almost every window.

Plastic was on the outside of one side window. It was stuck on with three-quarter inch waterproof black electrical tape to provide a weather seal. The tape on the bottom left corner was loose and the plastic was curled by weather exposure. Last year, when I visited, Mrs. Weeback told me of kids playing ball in the street and breaking a side window. I remembered this was the window she pointed out.

The blackened windows reminded me of houses in Colorado City, Arizona. On a Grand Canyon family vacation, a guide told us about the "windowless" houses, windowless to keep others from seeing in. Dad thought the guide was filling us with a crock of fish. We went 100 miles out of our way on our trip back and saw them.

But the Diangellos' house was different. It had a CB antenna on the crest of the roof, three 2x4 foot skylights and three cameras. Two cameras were under the eaves on the garage and the third was at the other end of the house. Floodlights were installed adjacent to the cameras. Undoubtedly, motion sensors triggered the floodlights.

Satisfied with my scrutiny, I took a breath and thought, "What next?" I remembered the Diangellos' 3 to 10 shift and extrapolated that they wouldn't return before 11 P.M. I fixed my first gourmet meal and dined at the window in my room. Other than a neighbor passing by occasionally, Devoreaux was dead.

An hour was consumed entering my analysis data in the computer. My file's name was "Mrs.Weeback's House". Then I titled the first entry "First night—Saturday 4 P.M."

Dozing as I finished the computer work, I lay on the bed and dropped off.

"Crunch" and then "scrape" knifed into my grogginess. I dove to the window. The garage door was almost to the top and the Hyundai, with its headlights and tail lights off, was half way into the garage. Floodlights were not on and there were no lights in the garage! Automatically, as soon as the back bumper cleared the garage door's descent path, the door started down. No light filtered through the cracks around the garage door after it closed. An internal house door slammed. It was a black-out operation. The digital clock on the night stand next to my bed read 11:55.

Wide awake, I wondered why I hadn't heard the Hyundai's engine noise. Thinking that I may have missed it, I determined to listen for it the next time.

In 20 seconds, three skylights blossomed. I continued keeping my eyeballs on the house and ears cocked for sound.

At 12 bells, I heard tires in the street but saw no light. A Cadillac Escalade coasted into the drive, completely dark as with the Hyundai. The passenger, a woman with a CB in her hand, stole from the SUV while the interior lights remained off. She left the door unlocked, sulked down the drive to a bush next to the street, and disappeared. I heard a murmured "All clear" from her direction.

At once, the driver exited, eased the door shut and walked to the rear. Without a sound, he raised the tailgate, lifted a stuffed cloth bag, lowered the tailgate, but stopped before it latched. He moved to the front door; the skylights withered as he stepped to the front sidewalk to enter. Skylights blossomed as he stepped in and shut the door.

Yes, this was not only a dark operation. It was silent. When the digital clock read 12:15, skylights darkened, the driver strode out carrying a heavy four foot box about as big as an urn would be packed in. He lifted the tailgate, very carefully laid the box down, wrapped it in a furniture blanket, latched the tailgate and squeezed back into the SUV. A radio squawked static and then "All Set". The shadow appeared from the bush to join the driver. I heard the starter and then the SUV engine as it backed out and silently drove slowly away.

Did I dream what I just witnessed? Before I could forget anything, I fired up the computer and made another entry in the file: Sunday 12 A.M.

My wish to see if the SUV would come back paid off. I stayed at the window and the SUV cycle repeated at 2 A.M. The only difference was that the box size changed. And I heard the driver say as he closed the front door, "It's okay. It's all there." The SUV didn't come again and by 4 A.M. I fell on the king, asleep.

Sunday afternoon came before I could awake from the land of the dead. Enjoying life's greatest pleasure, I devoured every morsel of another meal at the window. At 2, the Hyundai with a driver and passenger departed.

Later, as I thoroughly scoured the kitchen, I multiplexed my thoughts. What did I hope to gain by this? What could I do to capitalize on this opportunity? The list grew so I created another file, "To Do List – Mrs. Weeback's House:

1) Listen for the Hyundai engine noise.

   This one was easy if I was by the drive.

2) See the faces of the two Escalade visitors.

   Flickers of the street lights through the shrubs may allow me to see their faces.

3) Record the Escalade license number.

   The plate would be visible by light from streetlights.

4) Confirm where the Hyundai and Escalade turned off their lights. I would see the cars as they turned into the street.

5) Read their mail envelopes.

   Wait for a delivery day. Hope for late afternoon delivery. Remove and return mail after dark while the Diangellos were working.

6) Get the names of the Escalade visitors.

   I could only hope they would mention their names.

7) Peek into the house through that loosened seal.

   Proceed along a path in the next door neighbor's

yard, break through the bushes and advance to the window from the rear. Take tape if repairs were needed.

The first four could be accomplished tonight if I could find a spot to conceal myself along the drive! Taking action, I scrounged for dark clothes. In the garage, I unearthed all that I needed in the gardener's locker: a pair of black rubber boots, dark blue overalls, and a black wide brimmed rain hat. I would venture to the drive after dark and poke around for a hiding spot. While there, I could check the woman sentry's hideout.

Wanting some help with my plot, I phoned Amin and told him where I was. "Would you be able to stay a couple of nights, starting Monday?" I asked. "We will ride the bus."

After Amin cleared it with the adults, he said that he couldn't wait. His agreement made my day. As I hinted earlier, Amin had special training. Why? It was because of his father. His father was the intelligence chief in Iran, became the intelligence chief in the Washington DC embassy, and then moved to Seattle to be the coordinator for updates to Iran 747s. When the updates were completed, the family returned to Iran. During the time of the 747 updates, Amin and I had been school mates in junior high.

Being in the intelligence community all his life, Amin had been tutored in personal conditioning including sports, education, and undercover work. I needed his undercover work skills for what I planned for the next two weeks.

Fortunately for me, Amin's parents elected for Amin to

continue his American education for another year and arranged for him to stay in a local American home.

"Bring some dark clothes. We're going to shadow the Diangellos after dark!" I told him.

"That's my specialty. Nobody ever caught me when I took a class in it. I can't wait." And he hung up.

Preparing for the night adventure, I dressed in my spying uniform. The rubber boots were two sizes too big and I knew that they would make slow noisy going. Otherwise, I had a good disguise. With the collar turned up and the oversized hat, only my lips, nose and eyes were visible.

Waiting for full dark before I ventured out, I sat at the window and monitored neighborhood activity. Again, almost nothing was moving. A dog, an overfed Cocker Spaniel, sniffed its way, lifting its leg to mark its space. It entered the neighbor's yard, claimed the porch and meandered into the Diangello's drive. As it reached three feet onto the paved drive, light brighter than sunlight covered the area for a half block. Those floods must be 300 watts each. Mounted in pairs, I was surprised that they didn't blow a circuit breaker; turn-on surge current must exceed 60 amps.

The dog yipped and, with its tail between its legs, vanished from sight.

The floods remained on for 5 minutes. I was sure the cameras were linked to the floods and recorded the entire time. The Diangellos must disable the floods by remote before they drive in. Knowing where the floods were triggered by the dog, I was confident that I could avoid energizing them.

Afraid that the boots would slow me too much if the floods inadvertently came on, I did a room by room search and ended up in the garage. There was a row of fast-dry spray paint cans. I selected black, placed my shoes on newspaper and changed the white shoes to black.

Luckily I had started dressing early and after all the delays, I was only a few minutes later than I had planned. Sprinting through the back door and along the side of the house, I reached the street. I wanted to confirm that I could hide in the bushes next to the drive without triggering the floods. I crossed the street, paused next to the first bush to examine where the woman sentry had disappeared, and found her hidey-hole. The bushes had been trimmed to form a gap adjacent to the trunk and a folded camping stool lay on the ground.

From there I moved around the bush on the neighbor's side to a bush four feet from the garage door. Its base at the trunk was clear and a one inch limb would allow me to sit quietly. I would be concealed and yet see both the driver's and passenger's faces clearly. I raised my eyes to find the floods. The floods' aim was down the drive over my head and I would be in partial shadow. The sentry would be "sun" blinded if she looked into the floods to see me.

I retreated to my room to wait for 11:45. While waiting, I realized the risk in what I was about to do. If I were caught, it would be the end. I decided to wait one more day so Amin could be a back up.

Again, I sat at the window. Sunday night's events were a repeat of Saturday night's events. Again there was no engine noise from the Hyundai. The Hyundai must have been modified to be a hybrid, an impossible task.

Spreading myself crossways on the king, I dropped off thinking about Amin. Tomorrow night, we would tackle it together.

13 | *I Quit*

At 6 A.M, the phone woke me. It was Mrs. Weeback.

"You sound like you just woke up. Oh, I'm sorry. I forgot about the time difference. I'll make it brief. It's a murder trial and it looks like I may be here four weeks. Can you stay?"

"Yes. I'd like to."

"I'm sorry to wake you. I'll let you get some more rest. Goodbye." Mrs. Weeback was one sharp old lady. Brief? She said her piece and hung up! How can you beat that?

As soon as I arrived at school, I called a Hawk meeting for lunch in the orchestra room.

I opened, "Anything new guys? No? I have a bundle. "I am... " and I spilled the news.

"Amin is staying with me Monday and Tuesday. Let's do it in two day cycles. Sheila and Jel, you will have Mrs. Weeback's bedroom but to be proper, maybe the two of you should combine your two day cycle."

All agreed and would confirm after checking with their parents.

"The cycle then is, Amin, Juan and then Sheila-Jel. I've already been there for two nights and am not lonely. If there is a conflict, I can handle it by myself. We'll play it by ear."

The four nodded. Their expressions revealed how much

they were looking forward to it. Picking up our packs, we were on our way to class. At the last minute, I told Amin to take bus number 9.

* * * * *

Amin had a roll-around carry-on and I observed as we boarded the bus that he came prepared. Like me, as soon as we entered Mrs. Weeback's house, he climbed the stairs and strolled to the window.

After gazing out the window, he approached the computer to read my ledger and asked, "Do you have a computer password?".

"No."

The house, room and king didn't faze him. It must be old stuff to him.

"This is top of the line," he remarked as he read my notes and analyzed my layout sketches.

"There are 2 hours before we can act. Let's eat first, clean up and then suit up," Amin commented.

With 30 minutes until full dark, we parked ourselves before the window and planned our spy run. Amin would be the one in the driveway bush because of his escape abilities. I would be behind a bush in Mrs. Weeback's yard with a pile of rocks to throw as a distraction in the event someone approached Amin's location. We would be on site at 11:40. After the Escalade left, Amin would join me and we would venture to the window with a broken seal and peek in.

It worked as we planned. The quiet Hyundai approached, the garage door opened--crunch and then scrape--the Hyundai pulled in and the door descended. The Escalade arrived, the sentry posted herself, and the driver got the cloth bag and went in. On time, the driver carried out a box and the two boarded the SUV.

Amin and I met in the street and we followed the neighbor's path to enter the Diangellos' yard, 75 feet back. The presence of glowing skylight reflections in Mrs. Weeback's windows assured us that the Diangellos were inside.

Amin followed me and had nothing to say, unusual for Amin, and when I was able to glance at him, he was not himself. Something he had seen was in his craw.

We tip-toed to the window with the open corner seal and lifted the black cover. Flood lights remained off. After we both had a gander, Amin tapped my shoulder and motioned toward the street. We left without detection.

Back in our room, Amin captured the desk and sketched the faces he saw. He depicted every detail, far more than he could see in the dim light. As he wrote the color of their faces, eyes, and hair, I grasped that he knew them.

I reviewed my wish list.

The license number was 754WVU.

We had seen the car lights on both the Hyundai and the Escalade doused as they turned the corner.

Our peek in the window had provided inside details. The room was a bedroom with five or so boxes neatly piled according to size. On a table under the window was a splintered artifact with several brands of glue laying about. The room's door was open and a blank bare hall could be seen.

Although I had failed to put it on my wish list, Amin had seen into the garage. There was a furnished workshop but the garage was clean except for the Hyundai.

Our midnight jaunt had been 100% successful. All that remained was to read the mail. Amin would share about the Escalade occupants when he was more comfortable.

We both remained awake for the 2 A.M. cycle and then took our due on the king.

* * * * *

The other Hawks caught us as we entered the Commons wanting to hear of any news. Amin told them, "We've hit the jackpot!" but didn't have time to expand it. Without a meeting announcement, we met for lunch in the cafeteria. After Amin and I narrated our adventures, I expressed that the worst was over. There would be no more treks at night. A mail run was pointless and we would only continue the lookout at the window.

"I'm going to ask Agent Vera if she wants to participate after school today. Amin has another night and then Juan for Wednesday and Thursday. Juan, bring something dark to wear just in case. We ride bus number 9 and meet in the Commons." With these, my closing comments, the meeting was over.

As I left my last class to meet Amin in the Commons, I punched the Agent's number on my cell. She insisted on meeting me at Mrs. Weeback's to hear the story and was ringing the doorbell before Amin and I entered from the rear.

As Amin and I opened the door to greet her and she spotted Amin, her eyebrow raised. Without stopping, she traipsed to the kitchen, lifted the remote garage door opener from a bowl, poked the button and said, "Company's coming."

Standing aside to avoid being seen at the front door, I saw a Comcast van backing to the garage.

The agent put her arm across my shoulder and said, "This is unbelievable. We have leased a house, four doors down, for over a year to survey the Diangellos and haven't been able to discover anything. To be on their front porch is beyond comprehension. We have already contacted Mrs. Weeback and she authorized using her room with her blessing."

"Uh…" I was speechless.

"Sebastian, you have done it again. Thank you. We won't disturb you. We will only use Mrs. Weeback's room and her facilities. We will enter through the back. The van will leave after it is unloaded. Two agents and I will stay to operate the equipment and maintain three shift 24 hour surveillance."

Amin was still in his silent mode as we cooked our gourmet meal, cleaned and retired to our room. Relaxing on the bed on our backs, without talking, we stared and traced patterns on the ceiling. Rolling to his side to face me, Amin began to unburden his conscience.

"Sebastian, I've been stewing on something overnight and

it's not going away. I'm going to tell you in confidence because when it gets back to my folks, I may have to return to Iran.

"Those in the Escalade were my uncle and his daughter, my first cousin. He is not a terrorist! He is the black sheep of the family. He is a world known art thief. His latest known endeavor was the huge-scale plunders of three of Suddam Hussain's palaces when Iraq fell. He had a train of four semi-trucks which he filled and transported across the border into Iran. From there, the plunder was brought to America by ship which they use as a warehouse while docked at a Canadian port. Before my father allowed me to return to United States, he wanted me to know about my uncle. Akbar Bin Laden is his real name but I suspect he is using another. My cousin's name is Akhtar. I'm surprised to see her. She is devout in her faith to Islam and wouldn't participate in anything dishonest."

My attention was on the specks on the ceiling as Amin shared. I hoped that my inattention would give him the impression that this was no big deal and encourage him to tell all he knew.

"Uncle Akbar likes a cell size of four. The silent and dark operation of this cell has his trademarks. It appears the two Diangellos are the other members of his cell and that he is using the Diangellos' home as a distribution center."

"Amin, this blows my mind. What should we do? I don't know. It is certain that he will be caught with Homeland Security looking down his neck," I spoke with concern for Amin.

"I don't know either. I just don't want my Dad knowing

that I am involved and so close. To be frank, Iran doesn't care about the Iraqi artifacts. Their concern is that Uncle Akbar will be caught as a thief and be a blemish on the Iranian national image. An Iranian thief caught in the U. S. would magnify the problem."

Convinced that sleeping on it would help me think, I said, "Let me sleep on it. I'm going to check with the agents to see how they are doing before I turn in."

The door to Mrs. Weeback's room was closed. Without hesitating and knocking, I thrust open the door and strode in. An agent forcibly grabbed my collar and threw me to the far wall in the hall. I fell to my knees and as I recovered, he bellowed, "This is a restricted off-limits area. You stay out."

Seething, I limped back to Amin, saying, "They threw me out. Let's level the playing field. Let's eat again... I'm going to cook five meals, bake buns, and make a 12 cup pot of coffee to let odors drift up the stairs under the door to torment the agents. All they have to eat are WalMart cellophane wrapped sandwiches and bottled water. Want to join me?"

As we were swallowing the last morsel, Agent Vera loomed over our table. I could see her mouth working as she detected the extra three plates of food and smelled the coffee. Maybe it was time for some peace keeping.

"Sebastian, we can't show you what we are doing or finding but I can tell you what we are using. We have heat sensing equipment to tell how many and where each is in the house. There is a laser mike that records pieces of their conversations. The camera is infrared and is strong enough to read a book lying at the front door in the dark."

She saw my nostrils flare and my ears twitch and knew that she had made me angrier. I provided the house and all she gave back was a description of what they would use to obtain what I wanted to know.

"This has to do with national security and Amin is not cleared. Although you are, you are being asked to step aside to avoid a slip to your friend."

I was boiling like a tea kettle. Each bubble that burst made me madder. The kettle was whistling so loudly that I couldn't hear myself think. I was afraid I would swat her stoic face.

In my wrath, I spouted, "Don't you know-it-all, national-security-secret-game players with all your fancy equipment know how far behind you are? Sure, I filled you in on some of the things that you are to watch for but it's like the Daytona 500. Amin and I have traversed two laps and you haven't even started your car!"

The scars on her pink face were beginning to color. The Agent had difficulty containing her ire.

"Do you remember how nasty I was back there at Stahl and remember my apology? Well, I've taken the word "apologize" out of my vocabulary. This is going to be 'ugly nasty'."

1) Do you know who Amin is? He has done more for this operation in two days than Homeland Security, the FBI and the Pierce County Sheriff combined have done in two years.

The agent's scars were red now. Job slander was not her normal fare. With Ms. Webster's house access, she thought she was on top of her game.

I glanced at Amin and smiled.

He said, "Yah. Yah," and stuck his tongue out, put his thumbs in his ears and waved his fingers.

I continued,

2) Have you looked into Diangello's house? …We have!

3) Do you know the Escalade license number, 743WVU, and who it belongs to? …We do!

4) Do you know who the Escalade driver and passenger are? …We do!

5) Do you know what's in the cloth bag they carry into the house? …We do!

6) Do you know what's in the boxes that are carried out to the Escalade? …We do!

7) Do you know what they are doing with the boxes? …We do!

8) Do you know who bombed the Espinozas' house in Los Angeles? …We do!

9) Do you know who bombed the man and his dog in Los Angeles? …We do!

Agent Vera's face showed shock. The presence of a dog at the bombing was evidence that was tightly guarded.

After my tirade, I grabbed Amin and said, "We'll clean up, throw all this food out. You pour the coffee down the drain and wash the pot. These know-it-all goofs don't deserve good food, coffee, or our help."

The agent's face showed her hunger as we threw out the food. I was still angry but the kitchen work was giving my mind a break and I was cooling off.

As we started up the stairs, I threw one more dart, "I'd rather die in the electric chair than help you anymore."

"Sebastian, Amin, wait."

We took another step.

"If you don't stop I'm going to take you in!"

I couldn't let that go by. "I know why you don't move on the Diangellos. You have been building your empire for over a year and once they are in jail, you will have to start over. And, for the record, your 'take-in' threat doesn't scare me. I'd be thrilled to be taken in."

On the next step, I made a decision. "This is my notice. Being a member of the Homeland Security team means nothing if you don't accept my judgment. Find another patsy."

From there Amin and I went to our room. As soon as the door closed, I said, "Don't talk. We're going spying while they are busy figuring out what to do with us. I remembered something we haven't done. We forgot to go into the backyard. Let's do it."

We suited up, slipped down the stairs and left by the back door. We were past the house into the street where the cameras detected us before the agents had an inkling that we were out of the house. Trotting along the neighbor's path again, we entered the

Diangellos' back yard. It was about 10:30 and we had lots of time. The windows on the back of the house were not shrouded. With our penlights we peered in and saw into the kitchen, the dining room and the living room and were able to observe a workstation in the family room. Most of the living quarters were in view.

Happy with our find, we trotted back to Mrs. Weeback's yard. Agents met us, threw us on the ground, and handcuffed us. Soon we were facing Agent Vera in the kitchen.

"You smarted off that you would be thrilled to be taken in. You are about to get your thrill. I'm not about to let the operation be shattered by smart-mouthed cowboy teenagers."

Within 10 minutes, a black four-door Ford came and we were taken out the back gate and thrown in the back seat. Before they shut the door to lock us in, knowing that Agent Vera couldn't stand the sight of me, I murmured to her, "I'll tell you a secret if you'll come close enough for me to whisper it in your ear."

Her posture was rigid. I thought she was going to send us on our way. Then she bent to put her ear next to my lips and I whispered, "The back windows are wide open. You can see everything."

She jerked back as if I had tried to kiss her. She held her hands up, palms out and exclaimed,

"Wait, while I think." It didn't take long.

"Release them."

To the agents, she said, "You two, get your gear. You have about five minutes. The back windows are not covered. Go. Go.

Go."

"Sebastian and Amin, go to your room. I'll be there in a minute."

Delighted to be released, Amin and I did as she demanded. Again I shut the door. I wanted to share with Amin what I had decided.

"Your uncle is in real trouble. He may be a thief but I'll bet he has never killed."

Amin nodded.

"And I'll bet he is an 'honest' thief! Could it be that he is a thief who steals stolen goods and returns them to the original owners? Why don't we find out?"

Amin nodded again.

"I'm going to warn your uncle so that he can get away and not be entangled with the murdering Diangellos by association. With all the Homeland Security equipment actively studying what goes on at the Diangellos, after tonight, your uncle will be identified and caught with his pants down. Within a day or two, Swat teams will converge on the house and capture him. Will you help me?"

"Anything."

"We'll lock our door about 11. For exiting the house, we can crawl out the dormer window, walk across the roof to the corner, reach out about two feet, catch a tree branch with one hand, swing over and climb down.

"I'll conceal myself where you hid in the driveway bush

and wait until the driver is in the house. After the driver goes in, the floods will probably be enabled to prevent a surprise intruder. Then, you will advance on the front walk until the floods come on and take flight like a bear is on your heels. The sentry will see you before you trip the lights and alert them of your approach. The Diangellos will be rushing out the front door as the floods flare on so you may want to flee into the bushes of the neighbor's yard. With the distraction of them watching you, although the area will be lighted, I should be able to inch undetected into the SUV through the unlocked front door and ease to the back seat. I'll lie on the floor until we are well away."

Amin wanted to change places since his uncle and cousin would recognize him.

"Not the best way if Akbar is in touch with your father. Also, your skills of evasion are better than mine."

We were at a standstill while we looked for holes in the plan. As we thought deeper, we couldn't hide our grins as we thought of the reaction the agents would have when they saw our stunt.

Agent Vera opened the door with a bang. "I'm sorry that it took more than a minute. I have removed the lock from our observation center. Sebastian, please reconsider your resignation. We were wrong to shut you and Amin out and would like to know what you know. Will you share?"

Both of us remained somber faced without a word.

"Start with who told you that a dog was killed in Los

Angeles."

"Nobody told me; I deduced it. A solitary man was walking a half block from a park that has a dog walk, and the wife said 'we lost them both' to a reporter. I just put two and two together. Another person's death would have been listed in the paper."

The agent shook her head. It was so obvious.

"Tell me about Amin."

"He is the son of Abdul Bin Laden, Iran's Chief of Intelligence, second to President Mahmoud Ahmadinejad."

Agent Vera dropped onto a chair and stared at Amin. Trying to collect her wits and remember how she may have harmed him, she wasn't able to utter even an apology. Thinking of how the agents had thrown us to the ground and handcuffed us, she rubbed her own wrists.

Amin, seeing her discomfort, relieved the atmosphere by expressing, "I'm sorry for the confusion. You had no way of knowing. Sebastian and I are unpredictable cowboys and, without explanation, we are not afraid to tackle the right thing to do. Undoubtedly, we will do it again and you will be angry again. So let's put this one behind us as if never happened and start fresh. Deal?" And he held his hand out to the agent.

Agent Vera grasped his hand in both of hers.

"Thank you. You are my kind of gentleman."

I winked at Amin and knew that he had greased the skids for our next exploit.

14 | *The Ship*

Amin and I went down for a snack and had pizza and chocolate sundaes. This was Tuesday night, a school night, and we weren't sure we would sleep at all. Food would have to replace sleep.

By 10:55, we were suited and raising the window. The screen came out and was hidden under the bed. Hanging onto the eaves, we carefully stepped onto the slanted roof and discovered that we could walk on it. Everything fell into place and soon we were at the edge of the street. We hunkered down between two bushes and waited for our hearts to stabilize. Avoiding the Homeland Security systems by crossing the street a block away, Amin toured the neighbor's yard on the side opposite the sentry post. He reported back that the sentry would see him for the last five feet before he reached the front walk.

"Run those few steps," I told him.

"You didn't need to say that," he said.

At 11:45, I crossed the street two houses down and approached my bush hoping that the Homeland Security heat sensing equipment was off. The plan clicked like we had planned..

The Hyundai arrived and then the Escalade. As soon as the driver was in the house, Amin approached, was seen by the sentry and I heard, "Company's coming." Skylight reflections disappeared from Ms. Weeback's windows. The floods tripped on and the Diangellos rushed out with their guns sweeping the yard. Amin was spotted but disappeared into the bushes before the brothers were sure of what they had seen.

I was on the floor in the back of the SUV before Amin was out of sight. A CB squawked,

"I thought I saw a kid. Did you see him?"

A soft voice responded, "Yeah. He stepped from the bushes, ran for the front door, and when the floods came on, he went back into the bushes. The lights scared him off. All clear now."

The Diangellos left the yard and the skylights blossomed for a short period and then darkened as the driver brought out four boxes. The boxes were loaded and the driver and sentry anxiously boarded. The unannounced visitor had made them eager to drive away.

I flattened myself to the floor until we were underway. Able to raise my head out of sight under the head rest, I saw familiar landmarks. Tacoma was our destination. Akbar and his daughter jabbered without stopping but not in English.

When I smelled salt water and heard semi-trucks, I sensed that we were at the Tacoma docks. The driver slowed, turned left and drove up a ramp into a ship. As the two exited, I raised enough to see them ascend steps. Inspecting my surroundings, the ship was like an open warehouse. Columns of boxes, neatly labeled and stocked according to size, filled the area. Two jitneys were parked along a wall. A complex temporary computer work station was constructed on the wall next to the jitneys.

The hold was uninhabited. I climbed out of the SUV and followed the steps Akbar and Akhtar had taken. Two levels up, cabins lined the passageway. I walked and placed my ear to each door. When I heard Akbar talking, I knocked on the door.

"Enter."

I opened the door. Akbar and Akhtar were standing and drinking from porcelain cups. I smelled tea.

I smiled and said, "I have found you at last! I'm Sebastian Boyle. I know who you are, Akbar and Akhtar. I have come to warn you."

Both set their cups down with astonishment on their faces.

"Wait!" Akbar ordered. "Abdul has told me about you. You are Amin's friend. Is Amin safe?"

"Yes, but you are not. The Diangellos who you are paired with are villains. They are connected to a bombing in Los Angeles which killed a man. They have been involved in several illegal activities here in Seattle. Homeland Security and the FBI have been monitoring the Diangellos for several years but have delayed arresting them and are using them as bait to catch their controllers. At the moment, you are a suspected controller and may soon find yourself in jail."

"Controller? I'm not their controller. They are commissioned employees who make bank deposits for me," corrected Akbar.

I couldn't stop. I liked both of these two.

"Homeland Security is in the house across the street from the Diangellos with every piece of surveillance equipment you can imagine. Your picture and voice were recorded tonight and within a few days, there will be a Swat team raid.

"I know about the Hussain stolen artifacts from Iraq but Homeland Security doesn't yet. After the recordings taken tonight they will soon figure it out. At the moment, they suspect that the merchandise is coming across the Canadian border in a produce truck. Your ship is safe but may not be for long."

"Amin sends his greetings but doesn't want his father to know. He's afraid that he will have to go back to Iran if his father finds out. That's all I have.

"Do you have someone to give me a ride back? I came on the floor in the back of your SUV. Yeah, I arranged for the flood lights to come on so I could get aboard. Akhtar, Amin was the person you saw at the front walk!"

"I thought that he looked familiar. I wish I could have said hello," Akhtar remarked.

"Akhtar, would you take Sebastian back. We will be underway as soon as you return."

"Sebastian, Abdul and Olde both speak highly of you. I will also. I will not forget what you have done tonight. Thank you."

At Devoreaux, as Akhtar let me out, she came around to my door to say goodbye. She hugged me and kissed me and said, "You're a real friend. Goodbye."

I didn't want to let go so fast but she was spry and bolted into the SUV before I could say goodbye.

It was 3 A.M. and the house was dark and quiet. I sneaked up the stairs and entered the room. Amin was wide awake on the bed. I raised both thumbs and grinned ear to ear.

For an hour, we shared all that had happened. The funny part was that when Amin got back, he had to climb the tree and enter through the window since the room door was locked. The agents never missed us.

* * * * *

The next morning, Amin packed his gear and I helped him carry it down. We enjoyed our last meal together and he insisted that he help with the cleanup. As we were finishing, Agent Vera descended the stairs.

"Agent, I know that you three are rotating shifts. Please feel free to use the three unused bedrooms when off shift. Also, dive into the food. Ms. Weeback would crucify me if she knew that I was being stingy.

"I want to get along. Please forgive me for my outburst," I apologized.

She walked over, placed her hands on my neck, and said with tears in her eyes, "I want to be your friend. Yes, I forgive you and I hope you will me."

I winked at Amin and then dropped the bomb on her.

"For your information, you are after the wrong guy. The SUV pair is not the Diangello controllers."

The agent's face froze. The cowboy teens were interfering again. Amin and I left to avoid her comeback.

A muddy pickup was parked at our entrance to the street. Recognizing the head of hair on the driver's side, I started for the passenger door. Amin sensed he was walking by himself and stopped to see where I was. When he saw Akhtar, it was like a mother greeting her son, just released from a year in jail. Amin bounded to the truck and was onto the running board before Akhtar could jump down. It was my style of embrace, long and taut.

But I wasn't left out. Akhtar had one for me!

"Dad wants to see you two. He can't risk being seen since he is sure his photo was taken last night. He is staying on the ship. The agents missed me since I was hidden out front. We changed vehicles because they have the Escalade's tabs. The ship departed the dock as soon as I was back and anchored in Commencement Bay until Customs can clear us. It takes a day or two.

"You probably missed your bus so I'll take you to school. I'll wait for you after school. We are using an open dinghy out of Dash Point Park to board the ship so wear rain gear. What you are wearing now will do. Amin, throw your bag in the back. Get in; let's go."

At Emerald Ridge High, I asked that we stay a block from the school and that Amin's bag be kept in the truck, and waved to Akhtar as she did a U-turn to depart.

The Hawks wanted an unscheduled meeting in the orchestra room. The fast pace required that we pass the word.

"Amin, why don't you share?" I requested.

"After SEBie contacted Homeland Security, they moved into Mrs. Weeback's bedroom and are running the show. Last night the agents took photos of the Diangellos and the driver of the SUV. I'm sure that the driver of the SUV will be identified shortly. SEBie and I saw into the house. They are processing Iraqi artifacts. SEBie and I are meeting with the SUV pair tonight." Amin reported.

"Juan, can we shift your visit to be Thursday and Friday nights? As Amin stated, I have an engagement tonight. Is that a problem since the school bus does not run on Saturday?"

"It's okay. Jel can pick me up, SEBie."

"Jel, if you want to join Juan on his visit, feel welcome."

"SEBie, do you ever make a mistake? If Juan says yes, I'll be there and then stay over to be with Sheila on Saturday and Sunday nights."

"Why don't we work it this way? Juan, Jel and Sheila will stay Thursday through Sunday nights and Amin will stay the following Monday and Tuesday nights. Is that a plan?"

All were satisfied and nodded.

* * * * *

After school, Akhtar was bringing the pickup to a stop as Amin and I walked out. There were no hugs this time, just smiles as we accelerated off. Wind was 10 knots and it was a rough 30 minute boat ride to the ship. Dinner was waiting and after more warm reunions, we relaxed around the table.

"There are no secrets on this ship. The crew is a partner in my endeavor. I intend to openly share with you two and hope that you will feel that you are also partners," Akbar began. He didn't need to say all this was confidential; it was understood.

"With the dinghy ride, it's about 90 minutes to get you back. I'm going to tell you a story and when I finish, I'll tell you why. Then Akhtar will take you back.

"This all started when I was in Al Basrah, Iraq, just north of the Persian Gulf, as Iraqi fell. A local museum curator expressed his concern about raids on the Iraq museums. A secondary concern was the contents of Suddam Hussain's castles. The castles were furnished with items recovered in archeology digs and stolen by Suddam's henchmen in illegal forays. An Iraqi army general was preparing a raid of the castles. The contents of the castles belonged to private individuals and to the Iraqi people, not some general for his own wealth. Faster than the general could organize and arm a secret attack group, I had four semi-trucks at the castles, loaded and on their way to Iran.

"When the theft was discovered, the general raised a self-righteous cry that someone had stolen the Iraq's heritage. I was labeled as Iraq's biggest post-war enemy."

In Sunday school, I had learned of Iraq being the home of Babylon and the Garden of Eden. I could imagine the enormity of the heritage and the value of the artifacts.

"The artifacts and merchandize were loaded on a ship and moved to a Canadian port where I began making efforts to restore items to original owners. In some cases, items had to be sold and currency for the sale was sent in lieu of the item.

"The world is made up of crooked and perverse men, full of greed and illegal intent."

I immediately pictured the Diangello brothers.

"I first tried the National Museum of Iraq but the curator was like a cagey politician. The person that he looked out for most was the one who stared back at him every morning in the mirror. The two artifacts that I forwarded to him disappeared.

"The Canadian and American curators were the same. Realizing the value of these Bible rich treasures, I sought help in churches. Why can't Christians learn to keep their mouths shut? I barely escaped out of two cities after word leaked out. It was a lesson well learned. The general hadn't forgotten, had feelers everywhere, and wanted the prize back.

"From my brother, Abdul, who is aware of my moral quest, I learned of a business here in Puyallup that has a world wide outreach. The owner's name is Angeline Diangello. She is trustworthy.

My purse friend? Angeline? This is a small world.

"I have had success with my endeavor using her. She makes the contacts for the merchandize and gives me an address. I deliver the item and I know it is on its way to an original owner or to a registered, certified museum in Iraq. After the item is authenticated, shipping and handling costs are paid which I collect from the party who I deliver to.

"Although some payments are missed or late, there is never any trouble. The nature of our enterprise requires absolute secrecy.

"I was exposed to the Diangello brothers when I overheard their name mentioned in the Tacoma Natural Museum of History. 'The best off-the-record financial dealers in Tacoma are the Diangello brothers. They have a lot to hide and are incognito.'

"I recognized the Diangello name and by association with Angeline's name, I contacted and hired them without references."

This caused me to think and wonder how savvy Akbar was. He wouldn't have been able to reach this point by being somebody's dummy. Then I remembered that, at one point, I was on my way to turn over the $3,000,000 purse to the Diangello brothers. I backed off. I couldn't paint the kettle black without getting black myself.

"With cameras in most banks, I can't enter a bank. The Diangellos do that for me for a five percent fee. I bring the money to their house in an unidentifiable cloth bag. They have been honest and straight forward. We also use their house for small scale distribution of the artifacts. I had no idea that they had other entanglements.

"When we are cleared by customs here in Tacoma, I expect to go to Um Quasar, Iraq. Now that peace is established, I will be able to make direct deliveries. President Jalal Talabani of Iraq has heard my story and welcomes me back. He agreed to provide security."

Akbar relived the story as he told it. I could see the relief on his face. Akhtar was smiling at me like she was the princess in charge. Amin embraced his uncle and then shook his hand.

"Sebastian, I'm not done," Akbar rumbled as he continued. "Here's what I want you to do."

"I have recorded all this. Angeline tells me that there is an honest upright local Homeland Security Agent who she trusted her life with, an Agent Abernathy Vera. Would you be able to route the recording to the agent?"

Akbar reared back when he saw the shock on my face. He stood, circled the table to me and asked, "Are you alright?"

"Akbar, I just heard an amazing Robin Hood story which has involved risk to both you and Akhtar. Let me close the loop for you. Agent Vera and Angeline Diangello are both close personal friends of mine. I, too, vouch for Agent Vera. Yes, I can give the recording to Agent Vera and she will have it tonight. We are currently stalking the Diangellos and are staying together across the street from their house.

"Amin, do you agree? Can you stay another night at Mrs. Weeback's and help me sort this out with the agent?"

"You bet."

"It's 9 P.M. How about we get back, Amin? Ready?"

Our parting with these new friends was sad. Akhtar and Amin swapped family stories all the way to Puyallup. Both Amin and I were clinched hard before Akhtar let us go. Then she was gone.

An agent was waiting at the door as we entered.

"Welcome back, Cowboys. Where have you been?" came out more like a piece of spit than a question formed with words. Saliva fell from the corner of his mouth as he spoke. The remains on the table told why. The agents had accepted my offer and made pigs of themselves. Discards from five meals were scattered about.

Instantly angry, I spurted back, "Sorry we missed the feast. I hope that you didn't overeat and make it hard to stay awake for your watch tonight. I've heard that when it comes to eating, police like donuts, FBI likes lattes and Homeland Security is like a hog at a trough.

"Come on, Amin. Let's find Agent Vera."

Agent Vera was at the head of the stairs with a welcome smile. As I passed her, she commented, "I agree!" She followed us into our room.

Amin rolled his carry-on back to its rack and said, "Agent Vera, we have something we'd like you to listen to. Can you stay for a few minutes?"

"Be glad to. Just a minute." She went to the door and hollered, "Please do the clean up. I'm tied up." At once she sought a seat and expected to listen to a tale.

Instead of saying anything, Amin slipped the CD into the CD player and it started. When it reached the part where the semi-trucks had crossed into Iran, Amin stopped the play.

Looking like a three year old girl with a hand in the cookie jar and with a broken lid on the floor, Amin solemnly spoke with precision that made you listen to every word he said,

"As part of my training, I had a class on the American intelligence organizations. As I understand what was taught, there are the police for domestic care, FBI and NSA for domestic and national security intelligence and the CIA for foreign intelligence. Information is dispersed based on a 'need-to-know' basis. This information is defined as 'foreign intelligence' and can only be listened to by the CIA. Maybe we had better stop."

Whereupon, Agent Vera said, "As a Homeland Security Agent, I have the authority to hear it."

Amin, still with the look of innocence on his face, replied, "Let me see your credentials. We'll check." He winked at me.

Agent Vera unclasped her badge and handed it to him.

Amin inspected the badge, front and back, for two minutes.

"There is nothing here that says you have CIA clearance."

'We're going to get this straightened out right now. I'm calling the director of the CIA," and she put her hand in her pocket for her cell.

"How does it feel to have the tables turned?" Amin asked grinning so wide that it hurt.

"Before we go on, I need to give you some background. This is my uncle Akbar talking. The story is the truth of what happened in Iraq and how he is related to the Diangellos. He asked that you, Agent Vera, have this recording on the recommendation of SEBie and of Angeline Diangello, a person who I don't know. The Escalade is gone and will not be back. He and his daughter, my cousin Akhtar, were in the SUV and are gone. Gone? They are not in America anymore. SEBie and I met with them tonight and that is why we were so late returning from school."

"Can I ask a question?" the agent asked.

"No. Save it." And he started the recorder.

After the recording wound itself to a finish, the agent was shaking her head.

"You didn't know, did you? I pretty much had that all figured out. And I know there is a ship docked in Tacoma with an Iranian registry that is currently being held anchored in Commencement Bay awaiting a clearance from Customs. Customs are holding the clearance on my say so, Mister Smarty-Pants." She continued with her one-toothed smile, "I gotcha."

Grasping her cell from her pocket, she dialed a number and issued orders. "This is Homeland Security Agent Vera. Release the Iranian ship GSN 13498722."

Amin meekly approached her and then threw his arms around her and whispered in her ear. "SEBie says that you are first class. I agree. Will you let me be your friend too? Thank you."

Tears were flowing when she replied, "You two are the cream of the crop. I'm honored if you will be my friend."

It was midnight before it all stopped. It had been a long day that ended well for all parties.

Before I went to sleep, I was thinking, "Now we're back to the Diangellos.

15 | *The Principal*

The next morning, I told Amin that he should leave his carry-on since he would be back the following Monday. As we walked to the bus, he drawled, "There are nicer places to live with better service but this is the one I like the best. You can't beat the entertainment."

"The entertainment is over, so now you want to leave?" I sarcastically questioned. "I hope Homeland Security is disappointed too. Maybe they'll pack up and leave." We both laughed at that.

Knowing that the remaining Hawks would be with me that night and could be updated then, we agreed to bypass a mid-day meeting.

I was in my fifth period when an office clerk came in and laid an envelope, labeled 'Sebastian' on each side, on my desk.

Sebastian:

Report to Principal Finn during the next break.

Ms. Webster

My next class was a study hall so I was not under the gun for time. I delayed until the end of the break before going in.

The office crew knew me well and as my face appeared, they said, "Go on in. He's waiting."

"Sebastian, lock the door and take a seat."

Lock the door? Why not put the DO NOT DISTURB sign out?

"How long has it been since you were in touch with Agent Vera?"

People talk about starting off on the wrong foot. Wrong foot? We were starting in opposite directions. I let my eyes drift to the office windows as I thought of how to reply. Then I decided I wouldn't. Off campus events were none of his business.

"You don't trust me, do you?"

I held my gaze on that beautiful Seattle gray sky and waited.

"Sebastian, look at me."

He can't tell me what to eat and I wasn't about to let him tell me where to look. Sensing that I would not respond, he began to lose his cool. He grabbed his coffee mug, half full, emptied it in three swallows, and jammed it back to the desk. Momentum caused it to tip, then fall on its side and roll to the edge of the desk. I turned from the windows and watched, fascinated by its spinning path, and then realized it would go over. I leaned to catch it as it dropped but missed. It crashed to the floor and broke.

"You broke my cup! You deliberately waited until it went over the edge to catch it," he shouted.

Two seconds were all it took. Yes, I waited two seconds

but not on purpose. And I had tried to catch it.

The clock stopped in that office for two minutes. Then he spoke,

"I'm sorry. I lost my cool. Please forgive me.

"Sebastian, Mrs. Trimbell has accused you of stealing!"

My head elevated from looking down at the broken cup and my eyes studied his face to see if he was serious. Mrs. Trimbell was my 4th period English teacher. There was nothing that she had that I wouldn't find a waste can for.

I analyzed our relationship, teacher to student. Without question she was an authority on English, could write the book. But my papers were never right. If nothing was wrong, she would criticize the way I signed my name. To me, she was like a weasel with sharp teeth. No, there was no love lost between us and now this.

"She reported that you took her 'good-luck' charm. Her mother gave it to her when she was 13 and she has kept it with her every minute ever since. Tell me what happened in her class."

I went over the details in my mind trying to understand why I was suspect.

"When I reached the door to the room, she was pawing through her purse like a dog digging for a bone. Stuff from the purse was haphazardly spread on her desk. As I stepped in, she upended her purse and shook it like it had been bad. Several things fell out and rolled off onto the floor. I stooped and picked up two small bottles: Tylenol and Tums.

"She screamed, 'Don't touch my things.' She was upset to put it mildly."

Recalling the surroundings, I remembered that I was the only one close to her desk. I would be the suspect for anything that was missing. And with the way she had chucked her personal effects around, there would be other items missing. I would be accused of taking those too.

"I didn't take her whatever. I don't even know what it is. And I don't want it."

"Empty your pockets on the table," he ordered.

Carefully, I dumped my pockets and turned them inside out, except for the one which had the Homeland Security pad. The principal asked that I stand at attention and he patted me down. Finding the Homeland Security pad, he jerked it from my pocket.

"I told you to dump all your pockets. What's this? A Homeland Security pad?

He turned a page and his gaze flickered over SEBie 1, Sheila 2...It was as though a lightening bolt had grounded right through him. He saw and understood something.

"And this doodling?   Tu 7:10 bus, We 7:10 bus, We 12:11 dead end?"

I clammed up and my grave expression conveyed to him that there would be no more answers. I swiped at the pad but missed.

"You want this? I'm keeping the pad until you are willing to talk."

"That's my personal property and I'll have the police on you for harassing a student," I bawled at the top of my voice. An assistant principal ruptured the office door lock as he clamored in. Principal Finn waved him away.

Heat from anger hit my head as an exploding mountain of C4.

"Fine, you keep it. Play your 'keep-away' game. It won't mean anything to you since you can't read the code." Not waiting for permission, I wheeled and left the office leaving items from my pockets on the table.

I felt as if I had been a car that went through its first automatic car wash. I had been ushered in by demand as if on a conveyer belt, swabbed with soap, water and bristles and then blown dry with a burst of hot air. The wash had sanitized my pockets.

After school, Sheila, Jel and Juan joined me with their bags on the bus and we surprised the agents. Jel and Juan embraced Agent Vera which lightened the atmosphere.

"I know you, Sheila. Sebastian hasn't said a word but it is all revealed with the way he looks at you. Welcome to all of you. This will be the agents' last night since things have simmered to a stop. Don't be afraid of us." Again names of the other agents were not revealed.

Sheila was an Agent Vera fan following the "he looks at you" comment.

After I conducted a tour, clarified which room was Jel and

Sheila's, then pointed to the king and told Juan that was ours, the four of us retired to my room. I exclaimed what had happened the night before. The three listened to Akbar's record and were thrilled with the escape of Amin's uncle and cousin.

We decided to continue the Diangello watch, particularly after the agents left. When conversation slowed, I told of my day.

"I hit a snag today. To unravel it, I need some help from all of you. Mrs. Trimbell lost a trinket and told the principal that I had taken it. He called me in and made me empty my pockets. When he detected the Homeland Security pad he wanted to know what it was and when I wouldn't tell him, he kept it. It's in the school safe.

"Sheila, do you have access to the safe? No? Do they lock the safe during the day? Yes? A person can't walk in and open the safe?"

Sheila was shaking her head. "No way. It's locked and there is always someone in the office."

"Sheila, what period is your office duty?"

"Fifth, for the next two weeks."

"How many of the staff are in the office?"

"Just an assistant principal and I are at the counter. If an emergency arises, the assistant goes out to aid at the emergency.

"If there is a student fight, who goes out?"

"The principal and an assistant always go out from their offices."

"What would happen if there were a fight and a fire at the

same time? "

"Last time, when there was a fire, the principal took two assistants and went to the fire. It's in the instruction manual. Then if there is a concurrent fight, the remaining assistant at the counter goes out to handle it. We are all briefed at length on emergency procedures. I am left to answer phones and serve the counter by myself."

"Sheila, does the principal leave his laptop on his desk all the time? I've seen it there every time I have been there."

Sheila knew where I was going. She dipped her chin. The others were beginning to catch up.

"During fifth period tomorrow, we're going to give the principal a dose of his own medicine. He will find out that if he plays with fire, he will be burnt. Here is how.

"Tomorrow, I will use a gallon of gas out of Mrs. Weeback's garage and pour it into that dumpster out close to the football field. Its isolation will prevent a fire spreading. With the bush cover, I can easily reach it without being seen. Ten minutes into fifth period, I'll toss in a book of lighted matches. Since the dumpster is half full, it'll smoke like a pile of burning rubber tires. The dumpster is way out there by itself and hard to see. If someone hasn't seen the fire and tripped the alarm, I'll trip it on my way in.

"Juan, when you hear the fire alarm, I want you to start a fight, a serious one. When they manage to pull you two apart, claim that the other guy is a raciest, that he called you a Diego. I know you are Spanish American and should not be called a Diego. I hope you don't end up hurt."

"I know how to fight. It's a way of life in Los Angeles."

"Jel, here's my cell phone. At the same time, I want you to call the office and dictate a bunch of credible stuff to keep Sheila busy on the phone. A list of student names and home phone numbers would work.

"Sheila, you will be busy taking notes with your back turned, and you won't see me come in and take the principal's laptop. I'll leave a note on the principal's desk.

"That's all it takes," I finished.

"What's in the note?" they said together.

"Please don't laugh. Here it is,"

PRINCIPAL FINN:

    I GOT YOUR BABY. IF YOU WANT TO

    TO SEE IT AGAIN, GIVE BACK THE PAD.

                      Sebastian

They laughed.

Just before dusk, I told the agents that I was going to show the three around the Diangellos'. On our sightsee, we stopped at the sentry post; the camping stool still lay on the ground. After examining where Amin and I had hidden, we strolled across the front and down the side to the window with the outside cover. I gripped Jel's arms and positioned her to block the view of the agents.

Smiling, I said, "Do you want to give the agents some excitement on their last night?"

Sheila nodded agreement right away. Jel and Juan weren't so sure.

"If we can make the Diangellos talk and reveal who they are working with, would it be worth it?" I inquired. They agreed but Juan asked,

"Do we have to be out here to hear them?"

"No. The agents have equipment that can hear a whisper."

Using my sleeve as a glove, I grasped the loose corner and ripped the sealed cover from the window, wadded it into a ball and dropped it to the ground. It was an insulated window. The upper half of the outer pane was splintered. I handed a tape dispenser to Sheila and said, "Here goes."

Unfolding a quarter-folded paper that was in my pocket, I asked Sheila to help press and flatten it to the window. Not sure whether the printing should point out or in, I rotated it back and forth. Jel said that it had to be placed to be read from the inside. Not knowing if the Diangellos had fingerprint detection capabilities, I wiped the fingerprints from the front side of the paper and held it for Sheila to tape it to the window. After it was attached, the trio were smiling with me and imagining the circus this would trigger.

THIS IS YOUR FIRST CLUE. THE NEXT CLUE
IS IN THE FRONT YARD AND WILL TELL YOU
WHERE TO LOOK FOR THE LAST CLUE. THE
LAST CLUE WILL TELL YOU HOW MUCH WE
KNOW ABOUT YOU.   IF YOU MISS ANY OF
THE CLUES, LOOK UP. I'LL BE WATCHING.

A friendly Iraqi neighbor

I handed Juan a damp paper towel and instructed him to wipe the whole window and the notice to clear the fingerprints. From there, we rounded the corner to the back to view the innards of the house.   Sheila wasn't looking into the house but was studying the trees across the back.

"They're like huge Christmas trees but I see a cave back there," she observed. I wondered if it was another sentry post.

When returning to Mrs. Weeback's, an agent met us and wanted to know, "See anything?"

"Yeah, and the Diangellos will too when they come tonight," I hinted as I ran up the stairs to my room.

The hours stretched out as we waited for the spectacle to start.   By 11:30, we had arranged our chairs and each was comfortable with an unobstructed view.   We expected the performance to last an hour.

Right on time the Hyundai appeared and the occupants repeated their regular pattern. Skylights blossomed but within five minutes they blackened. One of the agents shouted,

"Hey you guys. Get in here."

As he shouted, footfalls raced in the hall. Within seconds, the Diangellos sprinted from the front door, each with a large spot in one hand and a pistol in the other. They flashed the spots all over but always ended each cycle by pointing the spot into the sky.

After 15 minutes of wild searching, one went back into the house. We could see the white of the notice from the flashlight as he read it again. He came out and the two organized their hunt into four foot squares, side by side across the yard. Six sweeps surveyed all there was in the yard. The tall one lifted the short one to his shoulders and they scanned the tops of the shrubbery and along the eaves of the house. They would stop and rest sitting on their front step and set their flashlights pointing in the sky. Finally, one had the bright idea that more light would help and turned on the floods. With pistols laid on the porch, one aimed the spots while the other bent and pushed shrub branches aside and thoroughly conducted the underbrush search again.

We four were not laughing but listening for when they would lose their temper and start yelling, a time when letting something slip was most likely. But they had not even talked. My bright idea didn't bear fruit. After two hours of probing every nook and cranny, they went into the garage and brought out scissors, tape and a garbage bag. The notice was removed and the window was resealed.

Seeing them go into the house, we knew the show was over. We separated for our rooms. Juan and I lay quiet for awhile and I heard him sleeping within a couple of minutes.

The next morning Agent Vera came to me and said, "We've decided that we need to stay for awhile. I hope that you enjoy our company."

We traipsed to the bus stop and prepared for school with our minds dreading fifth period.

At school, quick like, in the 10 minutes I had before class, I stole to the dumpster and saturated the contents with gas. Coming in from my outside venture, I caught Amin. Knowing that he shared a morning class with Juan, I told him to be sure to see Juan in class. Each time I passed one of the plotters in the hall, I detected a paleness in their faces that was growing whiter. I hoped that when the activity commenced, their complexions would return to normal for it was a dead give way if it didn't.

During fifth period, it was as if we were producing a TV show. Everything worked on schedule and we were back in class with innocent looks on our faces.

Only one complication arose. Juan had selected the biggest boy in the classroom, a bully who had picked Juan as his patsy since school started. Juan gave him a note calling him a pansy without any underwear. The bully dove from his seat, stepped on a seat of a desk and dropped down on Juan. Juan had seen what was coming, prepared for the onslaught and drove his fist into the boy's chin. As the boy fell, he hit his head on a seatback and collapsed onto the floor, out cold. Juan confiscated the note and everybody blamed the bully, pleased that he had finally gotten his due.

Waiting for the boom to fall, I couldn't sit still. Without knocking, Sheila arrived, came to my seat, and announced, "Come with me. Principal Finn is waiting."

Knowing that classmates, as well as the teacher, had heard, I departed on her heels.

In the hall, she said, "He is so mad that he can't say his words clearly. You will probably be expelled."

Approaching the door of the office where the assistant principle could see me, I stopped and said,

"Wait a minute. I've changed my mind. Tell Papa Bear that I'm not coming onto his turf to be interrogated and strip-searched again. Also tell him that I'm not ready to talk until I can finish copying his files. I'm going back to class."

"You're crazy. He'll blow his top."

"That's what I want," I replied as I gently clasped her hand and then spun towards my class. A custodian's service cart was along the wall, 40 feet down the hall. I hunched behind it.

Two minutes later, the principal steam-rolled from the office, muttering curses to himself as he went by. I skipped the remainder of the class. Classmates told me of the principal's blustering entrance and his request for me. He had not believed when he was told 'Sebastian hasn't come back' and searched the room. He was swearing as he left. The principal's exit was followed by a buzz of excitement as if the home team had thrown an interception that lost the game. My classmates saw no hope for me and assumed that I would soon be expelled. I assured them that being expelled was not in the cards for me although I wasn't really sure.

I attended the final classes for the day and when I was on my way to catch bus number 9, I detected him watching my regular bus. I simply went down the bus row on the opposite side and boarded number 9.

Agent Vera was waiting in the kitchen like she had the goods on me this time. She was holding our Diangello window note. On offense, I attacked,

"Did you have a search warrant to get that?"

Somber faced, her eyes were like blue steel and it was obvious that she didn't intend to answer. So I braved another thrust.

"You said you were leaving. I had a bright idea and I wanted you in on it. I hoped the Diangellos would be so angry after they failed to find the second note that they would fight and say something. They didn't."

She continued to drill holes through me. I thought she was waiting for a confession and I decided to give her something to chew on.

"Do you want to see the next note?"

She nodded so I removed a loose leaf 8 ½ x11 from my notebook.

YOU DIMWITS! ARE YOU BLIND? I GIVE UP TRYING TO HELP YOU. THIS IS WHAT WE KNOW. A WOMAN'S PURSE IS UNDER A RHODODENDRON IN THE FRONT YARD.

Your friendly Iraqi neighbor

Aware of the purse story, Sheila and Jel were in stitches. Juan commented, "They'll excavate the whole yard." His prediction would prove to be true.

Agent relaxed from her rigid stature and expressed,

"That should hit them where it hurts and tie this thing together. Excellent, Sebastian. You may prod these two into making a mistake. If you'll give me a day, I can provide a replica purse and bank book. They were like cackling hens at a homecoming when they were inside after last night's foray. They fought over everything but didn't mention their controllers. This will really stir things up."

Surviving on six hours sleep the previous night, the four of us were exhausted and elected to call it quits and take advantage of the night off.

About noon the next day, Saturday, Agent Vera knocked on my door with a purse in her hand.

"There is a cement stepping stone, 10x16 inches, next to the front porch. It's hard to see under the rhododendron. It's the last place they will look. Plant it there."

I inspected the purse, a brown almost black empty Perlina leather purse. I felt the bank book hidden in the lining, accessible by a slit in the seam in the bottom of the purse. I slipped the bank book out and saw that it had all the information of the Cayman Island bank. The amount shown in the account was $2,932,317.48 as of November 1, 2009. An account number along with a phone number were listed. It was real and would have fooled me even though I had seen the original.

"We have our people stationed on the phone. We will confirm that the account owner, Angeline Diangello, has access if she brings correct credentials and can be certified by fingerprints and an eye scan. Electronic withdrawals are not permitted without rigid pre-arrangements. A withdrawal by an alternate will be allowed. An alternate person can be a legal representative, someone bearing power-of-attorney documentation. The alternate must come into the bank in person and provide three on-the-spot signatures which will be verified by a handwriting expert. The alternate will also be fingerprinted to allow faster subsequent access. The Diangello brothers have police records which prevent them from being an alternate. This will draw someone new into our snare. We hope that it will be a controller or someone closely tied to a controller." The agent was revealing far more than normal. Informing us of these details led me to believe that she had more in mind for us.

Juan and I made the trek to plant the purse and post the new note. A wet kiss fell on my wrist and I turned my head to the sky. As rain was starting to fall, night was falling fast. We had brought a flashlight, a shovel, a two gallon plastic bucket, tape and the note. I strained to lift the cement stepping stone and managed to roll it aside. I used the shovel to dig a hole for the purse and put the dirt into the bucket. Juan and I replaced the cement stepping stone. Juan was concerned with the disturbed bark. He used the back of the shovel to flatten the bark and make it look undisturbed clear to the next rhododendron. We removed the dirt smears on the stepping stone using the sleeve of my jacket.

Thoroughly inspecting our work with the flashlight shielded, we decided with the rainfall further masking our work, no one could tell that the stepping stone had been touched.

We completed the note installation in quick order. Juan grinned at me as he left our calling card, the removed piece of the garbage bag used for a window shroud under the window.

Agent Vera and her crew back-slapped us when we returned. "Good job! Nobody can tell it was moved!"

I punched Juan and said, "Come on, I'll show you."

I led him to a monitor that the camera was connected to. The stepping stone and surrounding bark were displayed. Juan punched me back and agreed, "They're right. Good job."

I threw my jacket in the washer and asked Agent Vera to toss it in the dryer when ready.

"Nap time. Two hours sleep. I'll set an alarm," I ordered.

I retired to the king as a hint and the girls left for their room.

The alarm woke us at 11:30 for the coming Diangello carnival, carnival because it would be much shorter than the circus two night earlier.

The Diangellos arrived and repeated their entry. The skylights blossomed and darkened within a minute. Edges around the garage door lit indicating a new activity. Shortly, the garage darkened and the Diangellos exited the front door carrying a pitchfork and a long-handled three pronged rake. The area around each rhododendron was rooted. I suspected that they didn't use flashlights or the floods to avoid alerting the neighbors again, a second time in a week.

The rooting lasted 15 minutes and they gave up. I anticipated that it would be a quiet night. The Diangellos were dragging.

The late nights were also working on our stamina and we were exhausted. I suggested that we forget it until morning and we all retired.

* * * * *

The agents were closed mouthed the next morning. The ambiance was that of, "I've been up all night and don't have the energy to answer questions."

That was fine with us. We could see the Diangellos in their yard half-heartedly nudging with their fork and hoe. As we watched, we heard through the open window crack, "We already did this last night. The back-hoe will be here tomorrow to do it the easy way. Let's quit."

It was a fun day. With time to capitalize on the luxurious facilities, we bathed, ate gourmet food, tried every gadget--TV with 60 inch wall mounted plasma screen, six speaker stereo, high-speed internet--and watched four movies.

The Diangello scene was silent. They left at 2 and returned at midnight.

After we witnessed the dead midnight panorama, I said to my mates, "Hold on a minute. This is your last night on this visit. I hope to see you again next Thursday for another four night jaunt. Are we agreed?"

Sheila, with tears in her eyes, ambled to me and answered me as no other could. Heaven came down again as I embraced her. She lifted her mouth to my ear and said, "This has been the most exciting four days of my life. I can't wait. You'll probably be expelled tomorrow and our visits here will be the only way for us to see each other."

As soon as we parted, Jel, also with tears in her eyes, took her turn. She said, "Sebastian, I love you," glanced at Sheila and then said, "like a brother. I'll be here Thursday."

"Didn't look like a brotherly greeting to me," grumbled Sheila.

Juan promised to come as he shook my hand.

"You don't need to carry your bags back and forth. Leave them," I offered.

16 | *Back Door Neighbor*

In the morning, my hands were sweating on my ride in the school bus. Sheila, holding my hand, knew of my trepidation. Subconsciously, a decision was emerging. A person can only take so much. I was that person. The excitement almost every night and through the weekend at Mrs. Weeback's had drained me of all vigor and now I was on my way to be expelled as soon as I entered Emerald Ridge High. I just would not take it anymore.

Sheila kissed me lightly on the cheek and said, "Good luck."

Sure enough, as I entered my first class, Principal Finn was standing at the door.

"Come with me," he demanded.

"Do you have my pad?" I responded.

"Yes, it's on my desk."

"I'll be right there. I need to drop my books."

"No, you come now. That's an order."

"Principal Finn, I drop my books or this is the last you see me and your baby." I retorted. I jumped beyond the reach of his long arms. "I gave my word and I will come."

He sensed my determination so he went his way. I had won round one. I dropped my books at my locker and picked up the laptop. Walking into his office, the pad was laying on the desk and

I exchanged the laptop for my pad. He arose, circled his desk, tilted a chair under the doorknob and returned to his seat.

"Sebastian, you broke my cup and stole my laptop. I've never had a student make me so angry. Saturday, I spent the morning with Hugh Campbell, Stahl Junior High's principal, and here is what he said, 'Sebastian is probably the brightest student that you will ever have. But I warn you, don't get on his bad side.'

"I managed, after some difficulty because she is in the field on assignment, to chat with Agent Vera. She confirmed your integrity and said that I might be burned if I tried a fast one on you."

The principal drew a conclusion from observing my stern features. He knew he had passed muster and was on my bad side and had been burned.

I remained silent.

"You don't know it but we are on the same side. You don't trust me. Why is that?"

This was beginning to be one of his politically correct dressing downs. I had made my decision and I wasn't going to back off. I would not take it anymore.

"You think you are like that spider in the center of the web and are able to jump out in any direction. You are not. You are like a snake slithering through the backyard. I know you are in the Diangellos' pocket and are their spy, keeping secrets and trying to fool everybody." I spit out my viperous venom and told it like it was. I stopped to see what he would do now that he became aware the truth was known.

"Wha…" and couldn't continue.

I went on, "You seem surprised! Here are the facts:

1. Homeland Security repeatedly recorded your car's presence in the Diangellos' neighborhood.

2. You interrogate and monitor me as well as the Espinozas to pass information on to the Diangellos.

3. During the office robbery, you wanted to know if the thief was a Diangello before the police arrived in an attempt alert them. Ms. Webster, Sheila and I all recognized the thief immediately but withheld that from you. I am not the only one who questions your motives.

4. Frankly, the theft of the disk pointed right at you. You knew what was in the safe and where the camera was. The assailant had directions on how to avoid the camera and where to find the disk.

5. You assigned staff to watch the Espinozas' lockers to see if they were hiding something.

"For your information, neither the Espinozas nor I are concerned with our safety. Homeland Security knows of my suspicions and all that I know. You would be the first they would come after if anything should happen."

The venom was beginning to taste bitter on my tongue so I shut my trap. I had spilled the beans and was afraid that I had said too much.

Shaking his head, I could see tears in his eyes. He was speechless. His jaws were flexing to respond but his mind wasn't in gear. His elbows moved outward and he laced his fingers behind his head. He leaned back in his chair in deep thought.

He'd better think it through very carefully because I wasn't buying any off-the-cuff denials.

Loosening his hands from his head, he placed them to rest on his desk. Bending forward as far as he could to emphasize his earnestness, he looked me square in the eye and said,

"I'm not going to waste time denying any one of your five points. I'm going to tell you the truth and you can spin it any way you choose.

1. The Diangellos are my back door neighbors! We have a fence and a stand of conifers separating us.

2. Two weeks after they moved in, a lawnmower was stolen from my locked garden shed. Over approximately two months, powered clippers and a five horsepower chipper disappeared. Hearing noise from such devices beyond the conifers, I, uninvited and secretly, visited their unlocked shed. My tools were there!

   Sheriff Deputies said they couldn't prove that they were my tools without serial numbers. The serial numbers had been ground to the frame.

   Deputies didn't accept that scratches made by jockeying the lawn mower and chipper past an extended bolt in the door of my shed as identification.

But they had their notebooks out and were taking notes when I bent some conifer branches aside to show them a tunnel through the conifers and a three foot step ladder on the Diangellos' side of the fence. They quit and laughed at my paranoia when they saw two birdhouses nine feet up.

3. I believe that someone high up in the sheriff's crew is dirty since no action was taken with this much evidence. I have been building my own case against the Diangellos. When your plight appeared, I wanted to combine it with my own.

4. The office robbery was even more serious and I didn't want to let the Sheriff Deputies excuse their way out of that one. I wanted evidence before they arrived.

5. Seeing your Homeland Security pad, I quickly deciphered your code and wanted to record it in my ledger.

"Sebastian, I hope you will accept what I have told you. I, too, would give anything to rid myself of my back door neighbors. Will you think on these things? I hope to hear that I can be a part of your team.

"I know that you set the dumpster fire and were the cause of Juan's fight. Footprints gave you away and a custodian discovered the torn note in a wastebasket. An imprint of your telephone number was on the note. With distorting the truth, taking Juan from class, setting a fire, promoting a fight and stealing a laptop, you have broken almost every rule Emerald Ridge High School has and I could throw the book at you. I also know the part you played in finding Lynn Whitney and admire your discretion in that matter. You see, I'm not trying to make trouble for you. I'm on your side."

"Principal Finn, you build a strong case. This will take some thinking. Also, do you mind if I share this with the others and Agent Vera?"

"I wish you would. I hope I can remove myself as a suspect!"

Our peace negotiations appeared to be well underway and a successful settlement would likely emerge in a day or two. With my Homeland Security pad in my pocket, I decided to leave. I removed the chair from the door and left. I was certain that no one had overheard.

The negotiations had taken the whole period and the closing buzzer was sounding. Sheila was waiting at the door as I exited.

"Did he expel you?"

"No. As a matter of fact, we made peace. He has quite a story which sheds new light. Pass the word and we'll have a Hawk meeting in the cafeteria at lunch."

At lunch, unable to believe what I revealed about the

principal, the Hawks digested it slowly. Amin was the first to make an appraisal.

"What the principal said is true. How would he know about the conifers, the cave that Sheila noticed, or the police stalling? We, too, have questioned the police stalling."

We agreed that Principal Finn was on our side and parted.

After school, I met Amin in the Commons. Both of us had our concept of how the Diangellos' yard would be changed. As we rode the bus, we anxiously waited through 14 bus stops; we counted them, before our stop. Leaving the bus we smelled fresh worked dirt. A trot through Mrs. Weeback's back gate along the side of the house to a bush in the front led us to what we wanted to see. The setting sun was low on the horizon which meant that blinding sunbeams sliced though the tall fir tree branches. Dust from the excavation swirled through the beams and decorated the scene before us with streaks of light and dark.

C&D Topsoil and Excavating were loading a backhoe onto a truck. Another truck, full of chips and towing a chipper, was idling and waiting for the backhoe truck to follow. The Diangellos' yard was completely re-landscaped. Rhododendrons were replaced with eight-foot wide swaths of fresh dirt. The stepping stone, hiding the purse, had not been disturbed.

Amin and I went in to question the agents if our scheme had divulged anything.

"No, nothing today. All digging and chipping was finished before the Diangellos left for work. They monitored every shovel of dirt that was displaced and each bush as it was chipped. Yard fill-in and leveling was completed without their presence," a disappointed agent volunteered.

"We'll leave another hint. I need to talk with Agent Vera. Where is she?" I asked.

"I'm here. I was conferring with my boss," she spoke at my back.

Agent Vera, Amin and I surrounded the kitchen table.

"You wanted to talk?"

"Principal Finn and I had a conference today. He took my Homeland Security pad and I snatched his laptop. The conference resolved the issue. But he threw new light on the Diangello case. He is the Diangellos' back door neighbor and has his own agenda with them." After I shared a brief of the meeting, Agent Vera agreed that the principal was on our side.

"Homeland Security has prevented the sheriff from making arrests of the Diangellos although there has been plenty of justification. The only burr we have with the sheriff is that there have been delays in the flow of information from his office in two critical cases."

Hearing that Homeland Security was delaying the arrest of the Diangellos confirmed what we already had concluded. But Agent Vera was willing to stir things up some more. "Do you have another note for our friends?"

Amin opened a book, fingered an 8 ½ x11 paper and said,

"How about this?"

> THE CLOSER YOU ARE TO THE FRONT DOOR, THE HOTTER YOU ARE. I AM WATCHING!
>
> *The Iraqi neighbor*

"Good, the Diangellos will get the purse tonight. They changed the aim of two corner cameras along with the floods and motion sensors to cover the sides of the house. The note cannot be pasted to the window without detection."

"We can go around the block, pass through Principal Finn's yard, enter through the conifer tunnel and paste it on a back window," Amin suggested. "You'll have to alert Principal Finn in the event he has a floodlight system."

"That's what we will do. Both of you will go together about 7 P.M. Call if you see floods and I'll contact him," ordered the agent.

By 7:30, the notice was in place and we were back in my room.

The Hyundai pair followed the same pattern and the skylights glowed for only on a few seconds. The stepping stone was lifted immediately and the purse was found.

Three telephone calls followed as soon as they entered the house, two out of area and one local. All three were intercepted by the agents. The contents of the calls were kept secret from Amin and me.

A message was sent via the Hawk chain to inform the others. "Purse was found. The next phase has started."

17 | *The Sheriff*

In 4th period, Sheila knocked and asked Mrs.Trimbell that I be sent to the office. When the door closed behind me, Sheila grabbed my arm and said,

"Trouble! The sheriff is in the principal's office asking to take you to the station. I overheard him tell Principal Finn that you wouldn't be back to school for some time.

"He said that the Diangellos filed a damage claim against you for destroying their rhododendrons and want you confined because you threatened to tear up their whole yard. They claimed that you broke a window and planned to break the rest.

"Then he used the Diangellos' first names, Ron and Wilbur, like he knew them and said that he had to take you to face the accusers."

"Sheila, I'm not going to that office. Here's what you do. Delay five minutes before returning to the office. Tell them that I was sick in class and went to see the nurse. You didn't find the nurse and me at the nurse's station so it looks like the nurse took me to see a doctor. That will give me 15 minutes to high tail it. Pass the word to Amin. Play it by ear on who stays at Mrs. Weeback's. Amin is there by himself the next two nights. I suggest that all four stay until I can return. Thank You."

I cleared my locker of its contents and, carrying my

backpack, I disappeared out the back door. I punched Agent Vera's number on my cell and left a message,

"The sheriff is here at the school to take me to face the Diangellos at the station. The Diangellos filed a complaint against me for destruction to their property. I think it is a ruse to kidnap me to force Angeline to impart permission to access the Cayman Island account. I am hiding at the first chained east-side pull-out on 128th when leaving the school. Please come and get me."

My cell beeped as I waited. It was Sheila.

"The sheriff was beside himself when Principal Finn advised him of your absence. I could tell that Principal Finn was relieved but he offered to call when you were found. The sheriff said not to bother; he would put out an APB. After the sheriff left, Principal Finn discretely called a detective friend on the force and asked if the Diangellos were at the police station. The answer was no and then the principal asked if any complaints had been filed in the last 24 hours. The answer was no.

"What could the sheriff say if he was the last to see you and you were missing after being in his care?" Sheila asked.

"I don't know. In the back of my mind I have been thinking that the Diangellos are using the sheriff as a stooge. He may not know that he is jumping into the frying pan.

"Agent Vera will take me somewhere safe in a bit. I suspect that activity will mushroom at the Diangellos' now. I hope that you four Hawks can stay on top of it." I kissed the mouthpiece and hung up.

The sheriff's SUV whizzed by with its bubble lights flashing as I talked with Sheila. His head was bobbing and his mouth was wide open as he appeared to be shouting. I wished that I had a police scanner to hear him.

Agent Vera met me with her one-toothed smile.

"Looks like the principal had it right, a dirty high up cop! With his connections, I can't use a safe house and we need to conceal you until next Saturday.

"I have a ranger friend, a teacher, who serves as a summer lookout ranger in Mt. Rainier National Park. He stays in a patrol cabin at Mowich Lake above the tree line by himself through the summer. Functionally, he watches for illegal campfires, lightning strikes and forest fires.

The cabin is fully furnished including a phone and an emergency radio. You will be comfortable there. The only problem is that it is a 12 mile hike in with 4000 feet elevation gain. The trail is well marked, even in the snow. Yes, the last 2000 feet of the climb may be in snow. The ranger and I are close friends and I often use the cabin to get away and recharge my batteries. Would you like to use it?"

"You bet."

"I brought a Homeland Security pack which contains survival equipment, the '10 essentials', in the event that you are caught with an unexpected emergency. Yes, there is a digital camera. The pack is yours to keep. I recall that you are a tent camper and know self protection in the wilderness. Bad weather is not forecast but you will be prepared.

I had dreamed of and would have given my eye teeth for such an opportunity.

"In an hour, we will arrive at the Carbon River entrance. The road is washed out and closed beyond that point. A map as well as an entrance permit is in your pack although you probably won't need it since it is off season. You will hike along the Carbon River Road to Ipsut Creek where you intersect the Mowich Lake trail. The Wonderland Trail is also there. Ipsut Creek would be a good place to erect your spring-up tent. It's easy, just pull on a black strap and it erects. It will be dark. Roll out your sleeping bag and crawl in."

"I've hiked to Ipsut Creek before and have seen the Mowich Lake trail," I assured her.

"The hike out is fast, down hill, and takes a short day. I will meet you at the entrance at 5 P.M. on the day that you hike out unless we change that by phone. Starting tomorrow night, your gang and I will be on the phone at 6 P.M."

We were on Highway 165 and I saw the towns of Wilkeson and Carbonado as we passed through. We met no other vehicles traveling either direction. The remoteness was settling over me as I realized that I would be the only human for miles. What if Mt. Rainier erupted this night as St. Helens had? Paranoia was my strongest vice. No way was I going to let fear rob me of this adventure. I closed my eye for awhile but flashed them open as we crossed a rickety bridge over a deep canyon.

"We're within a few miles. When we arrive, I'll hike with you about a mile to make adjustments to your pack straps; then you are on your own. Adjustments are critical and if not just right, you are soon sore with blisters.

Without locking the SUV, we unloaded and started on the trek. Twenty minutes later, Agent Vera checked and made an adjustment, patted me hard on the pack and said, "Have a good time. I'll be in touch." She turned back toward the SUV and jogged away.

An hour later I was at Ipsut Creek and started up the Mowich Lake trail. With the pack and climb slowing me down, I looked for a campsite. The sky was clear so I unrolled my sleeping bag, inched into the bag without removing my shoes, ate my rations, and slept under the stars.

In the morning, wishing for hiking boots, I rolled the pack to see its underside. There they were along with thick wool socks. Using the breakfast ration box, I nourished myself for the climb. Nine miles to go and I was ready.

Donning the new boots when I reached snow, I tromped through at two miles per hour. By noon I was at the patrol cabin with a wood fire going and was enjoying the privacy. At 6, Agent Vera called with four Hawks on a speaker.

Assuring them that I was having the best time of my life without telling where, I stopped and waited for the news.

Sheila started, "Principal Finn said that the sheriff was back four times. And he said Mrs. Trimbell was wearing her trinket!"

Juan wouldn't be left out. "The Diangellos drove by my house twice."

Jel said, "Your mother phoned here after the Diangellos showed at your house and she wanted to know what was going on. I told her that you were wanted, but you saw it coming and you vamoosed to a safe place. She seemed satisfied when she heard that Agent Vera was helping.

"I have another answer to a hanging question, 'How did the Diangellos know the Espinoza Family History disk was in the school safe?' Juan reminded me that Principal Finn gave me a receipt for the disk when I put it in the safe. I wrote our locker numbers and combinations on the back and one night, I had to use it at my locker before I left. I was carrying the receipt loose in my hand as Juan and I left the Commons for our hike home. A severe wind blew it from my hand at the dead end of 184th East. Juan and I looked for it for 15 minutes but never found it. The Diangellos must have found it because they parked there all the time."

Sheila had more to say. "We four are all staying at Mrs. Weeback's to be together until you come back."

Amin, my buddy, spoke last. "Don't worry, we have everything under control."

There was a pause as Agent Vera let them dwell on what they might have missed. Then Agent Vera dropped the bomb.

"The Diangellos blabbed last night. I'll list what is happening.

1. After the purse stunt, we know the names of everyone in their cell and their controllers. We have irrefutable evidence on each! There are three grunts and two controllers. The sheriff is the other grunt but they refer to him as a moon-lighting underling being paid for each service rendered.

2. The Diangellos tried to kidnap Angeline Diangello as she left her office yesterday while I was taking you to Mt. Rainier. That's why I had to leave you so soon.

    When the Diangello brothers blabbed, they mentioned kidnapping her as a means to access the Cayman bank account so the FBI initiated 24/7 surveillance. When caught forcing her into the Hyundai, they said that Angeline had missed three doctor appointments and they were making sure she saw a doctor.

    They were released on bail within an hour.

3. The Diangellos received the bomb formula from another source. They purchased the materials from four different feed stores today. Construction of four remote control bombs is about half done in their garage. They expect to have four assembled and tested by tomorrow before they leave for work. They plan to place them next to Space Needle, Qwest and Safeco Stadiums and King County Court

House Friday morning. They have airfare on Southwest 336/557, Seattle to Los Angeles, departure 10:35 P.M, Friday night.

4. The FBI will nab the controllers in their room at their New York City hotel Friday A.M. There is a team of nine agents watching them.

5. A Swat team will sweep the Diangellos' house Friday A.M. The sweep will be four pronged: through the conifer tunnel, broken window, garage and front door.

6. All will be charged and face prison. Clemency will not be possible.

"This is Tuesday. Would you meet me at the Carbon River Entrance on Thursday at 5 P.M.? I would like for you to be here to see the Swat team sweep Friday. It will happen just after dawn. You will be back in school Friday."

"Hey guys, I wish you could be here with me. It's a blast. Agent Vera, please call my Mom every day. She is a worrier. I'm sure that Principal Finn is aboard since you are using his yard for a prong. Thanks for the call. Good bye." I hung up before they could hear my voice break as I let my emotions take control. I loved these guys, every one.

I thought about the sheriff until I went to sleep. He had covered his tracks well. I had met him back at Stahl when the abduction occurred and he seemed to be a stand up guy. Then I remembered hearing about one of his children having autism with high medical costs and that insurance was denying his claims. Even though the Diangellos' financial rewards were needed to keep him out of bankruptcy, I was sure that he would refuse to participate if he knew what was planned. I needed to put a bug in Agent Vera's ear.

18 | *The Swat Team*

The last day of camping in the wilderness, Wednesday, flashed by. There was so much to see and do.

Early in the morning, I called Agent Vera. When I put the bug in Agent Vera's ear, she said that it was known that the sheriff was not a part of the Los Angeles bombing nor the Seattle bombing plans. It was likely that he would not even lose his job although he was moon-lighting.

The most exciting event on my outing happened that afternoon. Climbing high on the trail, I found a spot where it was clear of trees and the sun had burned off the snow and warmed the rocks. I stopped to have lunch and fell asleep. When I woke, I had company. I named him "Twin Peaks". I moved slow, took several pictures and watched him for 10 minutes. He, at least I think he was a he since he didn't turn around so I could see, was as curious about me as I was about him. I had never seen a mountain goat in the wild before and I wondered why he was at this elevation. He didn't move when I left to hike down to the cabin.

Spending my last night burning elbow grease and rebuilding the wood supply, I worked to leave the cabin cleaner than I had found it. I wanted to be invited back.

I couldn't find a garbage can for my waste so I used a plastic bag to carry it with me. Noticing odors drifting from the unsealed top, I inserted it just under the flap of my pack and let it hang out in the fresh air. My biggest concern was a bear detecting the odor. I recalled from somewhere that bears hibernate until April and this was too early in the season to be worried.

The climb in took ten hours and I figured eight hours out without stops. I departed the cabin at 8 A.M. to give time for side ventures. Bear tracks along the creek as I approached Ipsut Creek raised concern about the unsealed waste in my pack. Was I wrong about the hibernation period? To be safe, without unloading the pack from my back, I was able to reach over my shoulder, lift the flap and grasp the plastic bag of waste.

I heard a gasp and then a grunt. Wheeling, I saw a black bear plundering toward me as it followed the odor. I threw the bag across the creek and scooted as fast as I could with the heavy pack. Not hearing any more grunts, I bravely glanced back. The bag had landed in the creek and was floating below the surface in the current. The bear was standing in the creek with its nose in the air searching for the odor. I kept making tracks as fast as I could. I felt guilty that I had spent my quota on polluting the wilds. Next time, I would bring a bag that I could seal..

I arrived at the Carbon River Entrance 20 minutes early and nervously watched for the bear. Ten minutes later, Agent Vera arrived with her one-toothed smile. I jerked the rear door open, threw in my pack and jumped in front like the bear was two feet away.

"What's got you in a stir?" she asked.

"There's a bear chasing me!"

"You mean that one over there?" she said pointing to the trail where I had been.

"You don't seem surprised."

"She, her size is a clue of her gender, has followed me twice but has never gotten close. I think she is snooping but afraid. Every year Bear Management has to catch her and transport her to high elevations in early May. Scientists from several universities have been up to study her unusual hibernation.

The agent asked if I had seen anything and I shared about the mountain goat.

"Mountain goats normally stay above the tree line but will migrate lower, even as low as sea level along the coast. You were very fortunate to see one," she commented.

"Sebastian, some exciting events are occurring tomorrow. A courier dropped a written threat at the Seattle's mayor office. Here is a copy."

WE WON'T TAKE POLICE BRUTALITY ANY LONGER.
WE WANT 1 MILLION DOLLARS COMPENSATION FOR PAST ABUSE. PUT THE MONEY IN A SEALED WHITE BUCKET AND DROP IT OFF AT THE STERN RAIL OF THE SEATTLE VICTORIA FERRY AT 12 NOON. A SEATTLE LANDMARK WILL GO IF THERE IS NO DROP.

"Based on a description from the courier, who we have in custody, the timing of the bomb construction at the Diangellos', and a record of a planned helicopter rental out of Boeing Field for a short Puget Sound route, we believe that Swat team sweep will nip the threat in the bud.

"One of the controllers is an ex-Seattle jail convict who sustained permanent injury when beaten by a guard. He has tried twice to sue the city for his injuries and has failed. He did succeed in his suit against New York City for the same injury. The second controller was a Seattle jail mate. By the time the Swat sweep occurs tomorrow, both controllers will be in custody. Email and phone calls, which we have intercepted, between them and the Diangellos leave no question of their guilt. A financial record, that is, 'follow the money', is the evidence that will seal their fate.

"We have been able to put Ron and Wilbur Diangello in Los Angeles at the time of the bombing when death occurred, have the shop where the bomb was constructed, and have identified personal evidence from each of the Diangellos at the shop. A motive for that bombing was the same as it had been for the Espinozas'. The party that was killed refused to pay the Diangellos weekly 'collection'. The Diangellos will be charged with unintentional homicide. When an unintentional death occurs as a result of a bombing, the bomber is charged with 2nd degree felony murder."

"Wow, that is good to hear," I said, believing it was finally over.

"But it was your idea to get them talking that made it possible. After they dug up the purse, the Diangellos' tongues wagged like a flag blowing in a breeze. They recited the whole plan and who the players were. They even mentioned how much their payoff would be and what they would do with the money. We were able to connect the dots after that."

"I don't want any credit. Just get them off of my back."

"Don't you care what they were going to with the money?"

"No."

"You will. They had a down payment on a paddy wagon rental and were going to kidnap you and Angeline and force you to cough up the $3,000,000!"

"Me? Why me? I don't have the money."

"Angeline would have paid anything to keep you safe. Here we are. What I've told you is confidential. Please don't repeat it even to the Hawks."

Amin, along with the other Hawks, was there with a big smile when I walked in. Sheila was the first to greet me. After Sheila and I separated and I accepted the welcome from Jel and Juan, we retired to my room for an update.

Amin said Principal Finn had been invited to see the sweep. The principal planned to join us at 5 A.M.

They all wanted to know about where I had been so I told the mountain goat and bear stories. Each was amazed at my knowledge of goats and bears until I told them that Agent Vera was my source.

After a snack that I had missed for three days, we prepared for an early morning. Amin, Juan and I slept on the king. I was in the middle.

* * * * *

By the time Principal Finn arrived at 5 A.M, we were starting our breakfast. Without hesitating, he was partaking in the party. Then at 5:20, Agent Vera announced that the Swat teams were setting up. Watching their method of secret stealth, minutes passed quickly.

At 6 A.M., with three Swat members on each side of the front door, a woman advanced towards it. Floodlights brightened the scene as she proceeded to ring the door bell. From the agents' sound equipment in Mrs. Weeback's room, we heard the woman announce herself,

"I'm Swat Team Grabble. We have your home surrounded and are prepared to make a forced entry. Will you allow us to come in peaceably?"

The fellow at the door was in his long johns. He was Caterpillar Eyebrows with a pistol pointing at Swat Team Grabble's chest. The weapon began to drift and waver downward as a waterlogged towel sinks in a tub. Caterpillar Eyebrows was handcuffed before he knew the Swat team was so close. Only a few seconds were needed to bring out Hangman in cuffs.

Four bombs were found in the Hyundai's trunk, each with enough punch to take out half of a city block. Four large remote controls with a radio range of a mile were on the front seat. A

Swat member was heard to say, "They had four targets. They wanted to be sure at least one would blow and would be happy if all did."

As the excitement died, Agent Vera came to each of the Hawks, gave us each a hug and said, "You are on my team for life. We tried for over a year to do this but you five made it possible. Thank you. Sebastian, we are wrapping up this phase and your assignment will terminate by Monday. Homeland Security will vacate Mrs. Weeback's premises immediately."

My cell was ringing so I stepped away for privacy.

"Sebastian, this is Mrs. Weeback. The guy was guilty. The jury was only out an hour. I'll be home tomorrow afternoon. Anything happen there?"

"It's been dead as a doornail. I'm bored and glad you are coming back. I'll be here and will I be glad to see you! You think about 2 P.M.?" I don't think that I will ever tell the truth again.

"No later than 2. Maybe earlier. Goodbye."

I passed the news to the Hawks that the vacation was ending. Mrs. Weeback would return tomorrow. Seeing us lugging our bags, Agent Vera insisted that she deliver them so we didn't have to tote them to school. We Hawks said goodbye and started for the back gate.

"If you guys want to try the tunnel, you can ride with me." Ride with the principal? What would our peers say?

"I'll let you out in the street and no one will know."

"Deal." And we traipsed through the tunnel.

19 | *Epilogue*

On Saturday, Mrs. Weeback was as glad to see me as I was her. We hugged for a long two minutes. We were in her front drive.

"I know. You want to know what happened to the Diangellos' yard. Come on, I'll tell you a story that you won't believe," I whispered in her ear.

For an hour I talked until I was hoarse. She was so thrilled she wanted to make her home a historic landmark and erect a statue to Homeland Security. I expected both the principal and Agent Vera to come calling soon so I watered down my part in the fiasco. After she made me tell it one more time, we had dinner. When she saw the vacancy in her freezer, I thought she would dance. "It's gone. I don't have to throw all that out." Then she made me tell it again.

She arranged with my parents for me to stay another night. I watched her bounce up and down the stairs and thought Montana must have been good for her. The next morning, Sunday, she let me go when I promised to come and see her again. She insisted on a taxi.

It was quite a let down to go home after the two week high. But Mom, Dad and Sarah made me forget about the lows. Yes, I had to tell it all again. Mom cried, held my hand and repeated over and over, "My hero."

Sarah sat on my lap and periodically hugged me. Dad nodded his head about every third sentence. With them, it took two hours and I told the truth as it happened, even about the bear.

My lengthy discourse ended on a sour note, however. A distant whoop could be heard in the distance and was coming closer. Its sad song of dire warning, accompanied with what sounded like three fire engines, ended at our drive.

The doorbell sounded the Star Spangled Banner. Mom sprang off the couch to the window and screeched,

"It's a sheriff's vehicle with KING, KIRO, and KOMO trucks. There's a shiny state vehicle parked in the front yard."

In three steps, Mom was at the door and jostled it open. A man spoke. Mom turned to face me.

"It's the Pierce County Sheriff and he is asking for you!...Where did he go now?"

I didn't hear her! I wasn't there! My heart felt like it does when you can't catch your breath and my stomach was cramping because I missed lunch. At the first distant whoop, my sensors were grating every nerve end from the top of my head to the nails on my little toes. Trouble was coming. I was sure that the distress signal would stop at my front door. Without hesitating, I quietly stole from the room and made my escape through my bedroom window. I could survive indefinitely with my "10 essentials" backpack. Or better yet, there was a Devoreaux lady who would welcome me with open arms. She would be thrilled with the opportunity to participate in the intrigue.

As the clamor stopped in the drive, I was crawling through our back yard bushes into the neighbor's yard. Remotely, I heard the Star Spangled Banner and almost cried. I loved being home and regretted having to leave.

"What's the commotion at your house?" challenged me as I stuck my head out from the bushes. Hearing the sirens, the senior couple had been at the kitchen window trying to view the excitement through branches and between the houses. Upon observing me sneaking through the bushes, they both had rushed from the house to quiz me.

My first thought was to mention that it was a scandal but these people lived for real scandals, not just those they watched in afternoon soap operas on TV. It would require a time consuming response, time that I didn't have. On second thought I said,

"The Doberman next door growled at Sarah and Mom was frightened and called 911. Mom reported that my sister, Sarah, had been bitten to make sure someone would respond. Our neighbors fear that dog and have made numerous and constant complaints. I would guess that over 20 complaints are on record so authorities are hair-triggered. They came almost as soon as Mom called.

"My ride is waiting. I have to go. Have a nice day," I said and was on my way.

I knew that Agent Vera would soon straighten this out. Trusting my sensors, I was afraid to stay. Why take a chance on going to jail?

The Herald

Puyallup Herald March 16, 2011

Puyallup, Washington – East Pierce County

News briefs from around the region

STUDENT SUSPECT IN SEATTLE BOMBING ATTEMPT

A Puyallup Emerald Ridge High School student is sought for questioning. Two brothers, Ron and Wilbur Diangellos, were arrested for homicide in a Los Angeles bombing and were apprehended in an attempt to place bombs in Seattle. In a clemency move, the Diangellos submitted 14 year old Sebastian Boyle's name as the plot mastermind…

* * * * *

Agent Vera cleared my name in one day. My stay with Mrs. Weeback was cut short and our parting was sad. She agreed to let me go on the condition that I come back soon for another overnight visit.

My return to school was not as pleasant. The principal, Ms. Webster, Lynn and the Hawks were aware of my one day absence and were overjoyed that I was back. Teachers and classmates alike shunned me even though the Herald published a retraction the following week.

The Herald

Puyallup Herald March 23, 2011

Puyallup, Washington – East Pierce County

News briefs from around the region

STUDENT CLEARED IN SEATLE BOMBING ATTEMPT

Investigations have cleared Sebastian Boyle, a Puyallup Emerald High School student, of being a suspect in an attempted bombing in Seattle. Fraudulent testimony charges have been added to the string of charges, including homicide, against Ron and Wilbur Diangello. In a move for clemency, the Diangellos had submitted 14 year old Sebastian Boyles name as the plot mastermind...

After the first Herald article accused me as a suspect, my dad watched for a retraction in a following issue. When he didn't find it, he phoned the Herald editor, demanded a retraction, and threatened to sue. The editor, as if he had repeated it a thousand times, pointed out that a retraction had been printed on the back page. When Dad was finally able to find it, buried on the bottom of the page under a full page auto ad, he again threatened to sue if equal billing to the first article wasn't provided on the first page. The editor responded,

"The Herald has provided the retraction. You can sue but

others have tried and failed. The Herald is sorry that we can't do more for you."

Dad circled me with his arm and said, "We are big boys. We can take it."

Ms. Webster posted both articles on the student bulletin board and relations bounced back to normal.

* * * * *

As school ended for the summer and Amin came to say goodbye for a second return to Iran, he said,

"Uncle Akbar and my cousin Akhtar send greetings and hope that it will be possible to stay in touch. The good news is that their ship is docked in Um Quasar, Iraq. The ship had been unloaded and the artifacts have all been distributed to the proper owners. My Dad, Abdul, also sends his greetings and thanks. There is a medal waiting for you if you ever are able to visit Iran."

I knew for sure that this was a "forever" goodbye and I wept without shame.   We shook hands and then hugged like brothers do when one of them departs for a war. The remaining Hawks were also crying but stopped with a handshake.

Then as Amin parted, he gave me the good news. "Agent Vera says that Homeland Security has telephone access into Iran. It will be possible for you to occasionally call me from her office."

* * * * *

The Diangello case was transferred to a California federal court and we didn't get news of the trial. However, Agent Vera was able to collect bits and pieces of information. "The Diangellos tried every plea in the book but were sentenced to 20 years and the controllers, 10 years."

Revenge was not a word in my vocabulary. But when I heard "20 years" and I knew parole was available in a much shorter time, it didn't seem fair. I couldn't stand the thought that I might see them again.

* * * * *

Fast forward to graduation 2012.

The Herald

Puyallup Herald June 15, 2012

Puyallup, Washington – East Pierce County

News briefs from around the region

MASS STUDENT ENLISTMENT

This month, twenty four graduating from Puyallup's own Emerald Ridge High School elected to postpone college and started their careers in military service. Twelve were asked why. Each was quick to say, "It was U.S. Army Staff Sergeant John Newton's example that made us want to serve."

Staff Sergeant John Newton was a decorated Puyallup hero who died in battle in Afghanistan.

Principal Finn assured us that Emerald Ridge High School does nothing to promote a given career field. "Our program educates students to enable them to make their own career choices."

* * * * *

"Boyle, you're in the United States Army. The Army is your mother now. No more soft cuddles. Report to Personnel on the double," barked the master sergeant.

Double-timing for Personnel, I recalled that this was the fourth time such an order had been given. The other three times had been for record errors in my file: my dad's name spelled incorrectly, my enlistment date incorrect, and an incorrect marital status, married! I hoped that it wasn't because the Army had burrowed into my entanglement with the attempted Seattle bombing and wanted to do a follow-up investigation.

My paranoia was breaking out again. Would I ever be able to put that muddle behind me and forget it? Sweating, and not just from the double-time exertion; I pictured the on-base prison and what it would be like. Agent Vera wasn't available to me in the army and I knew for sure the direction I was headed. Taking a long breath as I entered personnel, I strove to control my emotions. Surveying the office, I didn't see any military police and my spirits began to rise.

"Boyle, reporting as ordered," I croaked to the desk sergeant.

"You applied for Officer Candidate School. Please see Lt. Helmholt, second door on the right."

ABOUT THE AUTHOR

Dean Hartzell
16902 91st Ave E
Puyallup, WA 98375-2287
virdean@yahoo.com
http://www.virdean.com

Born in Ohio, farm raised, Dean Hartzell is a Korean War Navy veteran, a retired electronics design engineer and design manager, father of seven, and a Pacific Northwest resident with spouse. He is the author of Changing The Rules.

13712228R00137

Made in the USA
Charleston, SC
27 July 2012